Lynne

The Secret His Mistress Carried

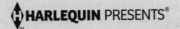

H HARLEQUIN PRESENTS®

Recycling programs
for this product may
not exist in your area.

ISBN-13: 978-0-373-13304-8

The Secret His Mistress Carried

First North American Publication 2015

Copyright © 2015 by Lynne Graham

HARLEQUIN®
www.Harlequin.com

Printed in U.S.A.

"Gio...you told me I needed to wise up when you informed me you were getting married, and I did exactly like you said...the way I always did," Billie muttered tartly. "I wised up, and that means not listening to a word you have to say."

"I don't know you like this."

"Why would you? It's been two years since we were together and I'm not the same person anymore," Billie told him with pride.

"It might help if you could actually look me in the eye and tell me that," Gio quipped, scrutinizing her rigid back.

Reddening, Billie finally spun around and collided dangerously with stunning dark deep-set eyes, heavily fringed with lashes. The very first time she had seen those eyes he had been ill, running a high temperature and a dangerous fever, but they'd been no less mesmerizing. She swallowed hard. "I've changed—"

"Not convinced, *moli mou*." Gio gazed steadily back at her, enjoying the burst of sexual static now thickening the atmosphere. That her tension mirrored his told him everything he needed to know. Nothing had changed, certainly not the most basic chemistry of all. "I want you back."

Born of Irish/Scottish parentage, **LYNNE GRAHAM** has lived in Northern Ireland all her life. She has one brother. She grew up in a seaside village and now lives in a country house surrounded by a woodland garden, which is wonderfully private.

Lynne first met her husband when she was fourteen; they married after she completed a degree at Edinburgh University. Lynne wrote her first book at fifteen—it was rejected everywhere. She started writing again when she was at home with her first child. It took several attempts before she sold her first book, and she has never forgotten the delight of seeing that book for sale at the local newsagents.

Lynne always wanted a large family, and she now has five children. Her eldest, her only natural child, is in her twenties and is a university graduate. Her other children, who are every bit as dear to her heart, are adopted: two from Sri Lanka and two from Guatemala. In Lynne's home, there is a rich and diverse cultural mix, which adds a whole extra dimension of interest and discovery to family life.

The family has two pets. Thomas, a very large and affectionate black cat, bosses the dog and hunts rabbits. The dog is Daisy, an adorable but not very bright white West Highland terrier, who loves being chased by the cat. At night, the dog and cat sleep together in front of the kitchen stove.

Lynne loves gardening and cooking, collects everything from old toys to rock specimens, and is crazy about every aspect of Christmas.

Other titles by Lynne Graham available in ebook:

CHRISTAKIS'S REBELLIOUS WIFE
(The Legacies of Powerful Men)
RAVELLI'S DEFIANT BRIDE
(The Legacies of Powerful Men)
THE DIMITRAKOS PROPOSITION
CHALLENGING DANTE
(A Bride for a Billionaire)

The Secret His Mistress Carried

CHAPTER ONE

THE GREEK OIL BILLIONAIRE, Giorgios Letsos was throwing the party of the year at his London town house. Yet, instead of socialising, he was answering his emails, escaping the predatory females who had dogged his every footstep since the news of his divorce became public.

'*I heard*,' a female voice murmured outside the library door, which stood ajar after a maid had served her employer with a drink and failed to close it, 'that he got rid of her because she did drugs.'

'*I heard*,' another voice piped up, 'that he dumped her back on her father's doorstep in the middle of the night with all her things.'

'*I heard*,' a third voice interposed, 'that the pre-nup was *so* tight she didn't get a cent.'

Gio was sardonically amused that speculation was keeping his neglected guests entertained. His cell phone pulsed and he answered it.

'Mr Letsos? It's Joe Henley from Henley Investigations…'

'Yes?' Gio asked absently, assuming it was the

usual quarterly callback to report a negative result, his attention still on his laptop as he mulled over the purchase of another company with the kind of concentration and enjoyment he would never find at any party.

'We've found her…er, at least I'm ninety per cent certain *this* time,' the older man carefully framed because neither of them would ever forget the mistake he had once made when Gio had gone racing across the city in his limo only to find himself looking at a complete stranger. 'I took a photo and emailed it to you. Perhaps you'd like to check it out before we go any further.'

We've found her… Suddenly, Gio was galvanised into action, springing out of his chair to his full imposing height of six feet four inches, squaring his wide shoulders while he flicked back to the emails. Fierce intensity had fired his dark golden eyes while he identified the right email before clicking on the attachment.

It wasn't a great photo but the small curvaceous figure in the floral raincoat was instantly recognisable to his hard, searching gaze. Excitement and satisfaction roared in an intoxicating wave through Gio's lean, powerful length.

'You will be generously paid for this piece of detection,' Gio breathed with rare warmth as he stared at the picture as though it might disappear at any moment. *As she had done.* She had contrived to lose herself so completely he had honestly begun to believe that even with all the resources he had at his disposal he would never track her down.

'*Where* is she?' he pressed.

'I have the address, Mr Letsos, but I haven't yet acquired sufficient info to make up a proper background report,' Joe Henley explained. 'If you give me a couple of days, I'll proceed the usual way—'

'All I need, all I *want*,' Gio stressed with rippling impatience at the thought of waiting even an hour, 'is her address.'

And suddenly, Gio was smiling for the first time in a very long time. He had finally found her. Of course that didn't automatically mean he intended to forgive her, he swiftly qualified, straightening his muscular shoulders. His wide, sensual mouth compressed in a manner that would have made his chief executives quail, for he was a tough man, an inflexible, stubborn man, very much feared in the business world. After all, Billie had walked out on him, was, in fact, the only woman *ever* to pull that stunt on Gio Letsos. But there she was on screen, *his* Billie, still wearing flowery clothes like a nature explosion, a shock of caramel-coloured blonde curls flowing round her heart-shaped elfin face, her wide green eyes unusually serious.

'You're not a very active host,' a voice remarked from the doorway. The speaker was as short as Gio was tall and as fair as Gio was dark but Gio and Leandros Conistis had been friends since their schooldays, both of them born into wealthy, privileged and pedigreed, if dysfunctional, Greek families and sent to England to board at exclusive fee-paying schools.

Gio closed down his laptop and studied his old friend. 'Did you expect anything different?'

'Even for you, that sounds arrogant,' Leandros countered.

'We both know that even if I threw a non-alcoholic party in a cave, it would be packed,' Gio said drily, well aware of the pulling power of his vast wealth.

'I didn't know you were going to throw a divorce party.'

'That would be tasteless. It's *not* a divorce party.'

'You can't fool me,' Leandros warned him.

Gio's lean, strong face was expressionless, his famed reserve kicking in hard and fast. 'Calisto and I had a very civilised divorce—'

'And now you're back on the market and the piranhas are circling,' Leandros commented.

'I will never marry again,' Gio declared grimly.

'Never is a long time…'

'I mean it,' Gio emphasised darkly.

His friend said nothing and then tried to lighten the atmosphere with an old joke, 'At least you could trust Calisto to know that Canaletto isn't the name of a race horse!'

Momentarily, Gio froze, his lean, dark, devastating features tightening, for that gag had worn thin years before he stopped hearing it. Sadly, not Billie's most shining moment.

'I mean…' Leandros was still grinning '…I don't blame you for ditching that one…what an airhead!'

Gio said nothing. Even with his oldest friend Gio was not given to making confidences or baring his soul. In actuality, Gio had not ditched Billie; he simply hadn't taken her out with him in public again.

In the garage, Billie was going through garments and costume jewellery that she had acquired during the week to sell in her vintage clothes shop. She was sorting items into piles for washing, repair or specialist cleaning while dumping anything past its prime. While she worked, she talked non-stop to her son. 'You're absolutely the most cute and adorable baby ever born,' she told Theo warmly as he kicked his legs in his high chair, smiled beatifically and happily got on with eating his mid-morning snacks.

With a sigh, she straightened her aching back, reflecting that all the bending and stretching had at least started knocking off a few pounds of the extra baby weight she had been carrying for months. The doctor had told her that that was normal but Billie had always had to watch her weight and she knew that while putting it on was easy, getting it back off again was not. And the problem with being only five feet two inches tall with an overly large bust and hips was that it only took a few surplus pounds and a thicker waistline to make her look like a little barrel.

She would take all the kids to the playground and walk round and round and round the little park with the pram, she decided ruefully.

'Coffee?' Dee called out of the back door.

'I'd love one,' Billie told her cousin and housemate, Dee, with a smile.

Thankfully, she hadn't been lonely since she had

rediscovered her friendship with Dee, yet they might so easily have missed out on meeting up again. Billie had been four months pregnant when she attended her aunt's funeral in Yorkshire and got talking to Dee, whom she had gone to primary school with although Dee was several years older. Her housemate was a single parent as well. At her mother's funeral her cousin had sported a fading black eye and more bruises than a boxer. Back then Dee had been living in a refuge for battered women with her twins. Jade and Davis were now five years old and had started school. For all of them life in the small town where Billie had bought a terraced house was a fresh start.

And life was *good*, Billie told herself firmly as she nursed a cup of coffee and listened to Dee complain about the amount of homework Jade was getting, which related more to Dee's inability to understand maths in any shape or form than the teacher overloading Dee's daughter with work. *This* life was ordinary and safe, she reasoned thoughtfully, soothed into relaxation by the hum of the washing machine and the silence of the children while they watched television in the sitting room next door. Admittedly there were no highs of exciting moments but there were no gigantic lows either.

Billie would never forget the agonies of her own worst low, a slough of despair that had lasted for endless weeks. That phase of her life had almost destroyed her and she could still barely repress a shudder when she recalled the depression that had engulfed her. She had been hurting so badly and there had seemed to be no way of either stopping or avoiding that pain. In fact, in the end it had taken an extraordinary and rather frightening development to show Billie a light at the end of the tunnel and a future she could actually face. She contemplated Theo with glowing satisfaction.

'It's not healthy to love a baby so much,' Dee warned her with a frown. 'Babies grow up and eventually leave you. Theo's a lovely baby but he's still just a child, Billie, and you can't continue building your whole life round him. You *need* a man—'

'I need a man like a fish needs a bicycle,' Billie interposed without hesitation, reckoning that the disaster zone of her one and only real relationship was quite sufficient to have put her off men for life. 'And who are you to talk?'

A tall, whip-thin blonde with grey eyes, Dee grimaced to concede the point. 'Been there, done that.'

'Exactly,' Billie agreed.

'But I don't have the options you have,' Dee argued. 'If I were you, I'd be out there dating up a storm!'

Theo clutched Billie's ankles and slowly levered himself upright, beaming with triumph at his achievement. Considering her son had had both legs in a special cast for months to cure his hip dysplasia, he was catching up on his mobility fast. For a split second he also reminded her powerfully of his father and she didn't like that, didn't go *there* in her mind because she didn't allow herself to dwell on the past. Looking back on the mistakes she had made was counterproductive. Those experiences had taught her hard lessons and she had forced herself to move on past them.

Dee studied her cousin in frank frustration. Billie Smith was the equivalent of a man magnet. With the figure of a pocket Venus, a foaming mane of dense toffee-coloured curls and an exceptionally pretty face, Billie exuded the kind of natural warm and approachable sex appeal that attracted the opposite sex in droves. Men tried to chat Billie up in the supermarket, in car parks or in the street and if they were behind a car wheel they honked their horns, whistled out of the window and stopped to offer her lifts. Had it not been for Billie's modest take on her own assets and her innate kindness, Dee was convinced she would have been consumed with envy. Of course she would have been the last to envy Billie's unfortunate long-term affair with the ruthless, selfish swine who had broken her tender heart, she thought guiltily. Like Dee, Billie had paid a high price for falling in love with the wrong man.

The knocker on the front door sounded loudly. 'I'll get it,' Billie declared because Dee was doing the ironing and Billie hated ironing with a passion.

Davis hurtled out of the sitting room, almost tripping over Theo, who was crawling earnestly in his mother's wake. 'There's a big car…a really big car on the street!' the little boy exclaimed.

It was probably a lorry with a delivery, Billie assumed, aware that any vehicle with wheels fascinated Dee's son. She unlocked the door and then took an immediate and very abrupt step back, astonishment and panic shooting up inside her like a sudden jarring surge of adrenalin.

'You're a hard woman to track down,' Gio murmured with supreme assurance.

Billie's facial muscles were locked tight by shock. She couldn't have shown him an expression to save her life but her wide green eyes were huge and anxious. 'What are you doing here? Why would you have wanted to track me down, for goodness' sake?'

Gio feasted his shrewd, dark gaze on her. Twenty four freckles adorned her nose and her upper cheekbones: having once counted them, he knew that for a fact. Her clear eyes, delicate features and lush mouth were utterly unchanged, he was relieved to note, his attention sliding inexorably down over her in a staged appraisal because he was strictly rationing himself. A faded blue cotton tee shirt stretched to capacity over her high, rounded breasts and his attention lingered there against his will, lust sending his libido leaping for the first time in a long time.

Relief rather than irritation consumed Gio because it had been far too long since he had experienced that reaction to a woman, so long indeed that he had feared that his marriage had stripped him of his essential masculinity in some peculiar fashion. But then, he would have been the first to acknowledge that he had never wanted any woman the way he had always wanted Billie. He had once flown her out to New York for a single night because he literally could not get through another week without her in his bed.

Billie was so worked up, so horrified that Gio Letsos had come looking and found her, that her feet were glued to the hall carpet. She stared at Gio, unwilling to credit that he was really there in the flesh in front of her, the man she had once loved, the man she had believed she would never see again. Her heart started to thump very, very hard and she sucked in a sudden snatch of oxygen, flinching as Theo drew her back to reality by hauling on her jeans-clad legs with his little fat hands to pull himself upright.

'Billie…?' Dee asked from the kitchen doorway. 'Who is it? Is there something up?'

'Nothing.' Billie rescued her voice from her convulsed throat and stooped down in a jerky movement to scoop up Theo, her dazed gaze roaming over her cousin's children who were studying Gio as though he had just dropped in from Mars. 'Dee…could you take the kids?'

Her voice emerged all husky and shaken and she had to force herself to direct her attention back to Gio while Dee put out her arms for Theo and urged her own children into the kitchen with her. The kitchen door closed, sealing the hall into a sudden claustrophobic silence.

'I asked you why you were here and why you would have looked for me in the first place,' Billie reminded her unwelcome visitor doggedly.

'Are you really planning to stage this long-overdue meeting on the doorstep?' Gio drawled, all velvety smoothness and sophistication. He was taking control the way he always did and it unnerved her.

'Why not?' Billie whispered helplessly, struggling

to drag her eyes from his devastatingly handsome features, remembering all the many times she had run her fingers through his thick black hair, loving him, loving each and every thing about him, even his flaws. 'I don't owe you the time of day!'

Gio was disconcerted by that comeback from a woman who had once respected his every word and done everything possible to please him, and his lean, strong face set taut and hard. 'You're being rude,' he told her icily.

Billie's hand clutched at the edge of the front door while she wondered if its support was all that was keeping her upright. He was so cool, so collected and such a bully, really couldn't help being one. Life had spoilt Gio Letsos although he had never seen it that way. People flattered him to an extraordinary degree and went out of their way to win his approval. And once she had been the same, she acknowledged wretchedly. She had never stood up to him, never told him how she really felt, had always been far too afraid of spoiling things and then losing him. Only a very naïve woman would have failed to foresee that naturally Gio would choose to walk away from her first.

Her abstracted gaze took in the fact that her neighbour was staring over the fence at them, possibly even close enough to catch snippets of the conversation. Embarrassment made her step back from the door. 'You'd better come in.'

Gio strode into the tiny sitting room, stepping with care round the toys strewn untidily about the room. He swallowed up all the available space, Billie thought numbly as she hastily switched off the television, which was playing a noisy children's cartoon. He was so tall, so broad and she had forgotten the way he dominated any room he occupied.

'You said I was rude,' she said flatly as she carefully shut the sitting room door, ensuring their privacy.

She kept her back turned to him as long as possible, shielding herself from the explosive effects of Gio's potent charisma as best she could. It wasn't fair that just being in the same room with him should send a shower of sparks tingling through her and give her that oh, so dangerous sense of excitement and anticipation that had once seduced her into behaving like a very stupid woman. He was so very, very good-looking that it hurt to look at him and the effect of seeing him on the doorstep had stimulated her memories. In her mind's eye, she was seeing the straight black brows, the utterly gorgeous dark golden eyes, the distinctly imperious blade of his nose, the high cheekbones, the bronzed Mediterranean skin, the beautiful, wide, sensual mouth that had made seduction an indescribable pleasure.

'You *were* rude,' Gio told her without hesitation.

'But I was entitled to be. Two years ago, you married another woman,' Billie reminded him over her shoulder, angry that it could *still* hurt her to have to force that statement out. Unhappily there was no escaping the demeaning truth that she had been good enough to sleep with but not good enough to be considered for anything more important or permanent in Gio's life. 'You're nothing to do with me any more!'

'I'm divorced,' Gio breathed in a raw-edged undertone because nothing was going as he had expected. Billie had never attacked him before, never dared to question his behaviour. This new version of Billie was taking him by surprise.

'How is that my business?' Billie shot back at him, quick as a flash, while refusing to think that startling declaration of divorce through or react to it in any way. 'I still remember you telling me that your marriage was *none* of my business.'

'But then you made it your business by using it as an excuse to walk out on me.'

'I didn't *need* an excuse!' A familiar sense of wonderment was gripping Billie while she listened, once again, to Gio vocalise his supremely selfish and arrogant outlook. 'The minute you married, we were over and done. I never pretended it would be any other way—'

'You were my mistress!'

Colour lashed Billie's cheeks as though he had slapped her. 'In your mind, not mine. I was only with you because I fell in love with you, not for the jewellery and the clothes and the fancy apartment,' she spelled out thinly, her hands curling together in front of her in a defensive, nervous gesture.

'But there was no reason for you to leave. My bride had no objection to me keeping a mistress,' Gio stressed with growing impatience.

My bride. Even the label still hurt. The back of

her eyelids stung with tears and she hated herself but she hated him more. Gio was so insensitive, so self-centred. How on earth had she ever contrived to love him? And why the heck would he have tracked her down? For what possible reason?

'Sometimes I honestly think you talk like an alien from another planet, Gio,' Billie countered, tightly controlling her anger and her pain. 'In my world decent men do *not* marry one woman and continue sleeping with another. That is not acceptable to me and the idea that you found a woman to marry who didn't care *who* you slept with just depresses me.'

'But I am free now,' Gio reminded her, frowning while he wondered what the hell had happened to Billie to change her so much that she could start arguing with him the minute he reappeared.

'I don't want to be rude but I'd like you to leave,' Billie admitted unevenly.

'You haven't even heard what I have to say. What the hell is the matter with you?' Gio demanded, shaken into outright disbelief by her aggressive attitude.

'I don't *want* to hear what you have to say. Why would I? We broke up a long time ago!'

'We didn't break up—you walked out, *vanished*,' Gio contradicted with harsh censorious emphasis.

'Gio…you told me I needed to wise up when you informed me you were getting married and I did exactly like you said…the way I always did,' Billie muttered tartly. '*I wised up* and that means not listening to a word you have to say.'

'I don't know you like this.'

'Why would you? It's been two years since we were together and I'm not the same person any more,' Billie told him with pride.

'It might help if you could actually look me in the eye and tell me that,' Gio quipped, scrutinising her rigid back.

Reddening, Billie finally spun round and collided dangerously with stunning deep-set dark eyes, heavily fringed with lashes. The very first time she had seen those eyes he had been ill, running a high temperature and a dangerous fever, but those eyes had been no less mesmerising. She swallowed hard. 'I've changed—'

'Not convinced, *moli mou*.' Gio gazed steadily back at her, enjoying the burst of sexual static now thickening the atmosphere. That her tension mirrored his told him everything he needed to know. Nothing had changed, certainly not the most basic chemistry of all. 'I want you back.'

In shock, Billie stopped breathing, but within seconds his admission made a crazy kind of Gio-based sense to her. By any standards, his marriage had lasted a ludicrously short time and she knew Gio didn't like change in his private life. To his skewed way of thinking, reconciling with his former mistress might well now seem the most attractive and convenient option. 'No way,' she said breathlessly.

'I still want you and you still want me—'

'I've built a whole new life here. I can't just abandon it,' Billie muttered, wondering why on earth she was stooping to making such empty excuses. 'You and me…it didn't work—'

'It worked brilliantly,' he contradicted.

'And your marriage *didn't*?' Billie could not resist asking.

His hard facial bones locked in an expression she remembered from the past. It closed her out, warned she had crossed a boundary. 'Since I'm divorced, obviously not,' he fielded, smooth as glass.

'But you and I,' Gio husked, reaching out to grasp her hands before she could guess his intention, 'did work very successfully—'

'Depends on your definition of successful,' Billie parried, her hands trembling in his, perspiration dampening her entire skin surface. 'I wasn't happy—'

'You were always happy,' Gio had no hesitation in asserting, because her chirpy, sunny nature was what he remembered most about her.

Billie tried and failed to draw her hands free of his without making a production out of it. 'I *wasn't* happy,' she repeated again, shivering as the almost forgotten scent of him assailed her nostrils: clean, fresh male overlaid with tones of citrus and something that was uniquely Gio, so familiar even after all the time that had passed that for a charged and very dangerous split second she wanted to lean closer and sniff him up like an intoxicating drug. 'Please let go, Gio. Coming here was a waste of your time.'

His hot urgent mouth swooped down on hers and he feasted on her parted lips with fiery enthusiasm, plundering and ravishing with a hunger she had never forgotten. Electrifying excitement shot through Billie like a lightning bolt to stimulate every skin cell in her body. The erotic thrust of his tongue into her mouth consumed her with burning heat and a crazy urge to get even closer to that lean, virile body of his. Wild hunger started a glow of warmth in her pelvis and made her nipples tighten and strain. She wanted, she *wanted*...and then sanity returned like a cold drop of water on her overheated skin when Theo wailed from the kitchen, jarring every maternal sense she possessed back to wakefulness.

Wrenching her mouth free of his, Billie looked up into the smouldering dark golden eyes that had once broken her heart and said what she needed to say, what she *owed* it to herself to say. 'Please leave, Gio...'

Billie stood at the window watching Gio climb into his long black limousine on the street outside, her fingernails biting into her palms like sharp-pointed knives. Without even trying he had torn her in two, teaching her that her recovery was not as complete as she had imagined. Letting Gio walk away from her had almost killed her and there was still a weak, wicked part of her that longed to snatch him back with both hands. But she knew it was pointless, because Gio would be furious if he ever found out that Theo was his child.

Right from the start, Billie had known and accepted that truth when, finding herself accidentally pregnant, she had chosen to give birth to a baby fathered by a male who had only wanted her for her body. There would be no support or understanding from Gio on the score of an illegitimate child, whom he would prefer not to have been born. She had only been with him a few weeks when he had told her that if she ever fell pregnant he would regard it as a disaster and that it would destroy their relationship, so she couldn't say she hadn't been warned. She had finally decided that what he didn't know about wouldn't hurt him and she had so much love to give their son that she had convinced herself that Theo would not suffer from the lack of a father.

Or so she had thought…until after Theo's birth when concerns began to steadily nibble gaping holes in her one-time conviction that she had made the right decision. Then she had guiltily asked herself if she was the most selfish woman alive to have chosen to have a child in secrecy who would never have a father and she had worried even more about how Theo might react when he was older to what little she would have to tell him.

Would her son despise her some day for the role she had played in Gio's bed? Would Theo resent the fact that although his father was rich he had grown up in comparative poverty? Would he blame her then for having brought him into the world on such terms?

CHAPTER TWO

BILLIE STUFFED HER face in the pillow and sobbed her heart out for the first time in two long years and once again Gio had provided the spur. When she had finally cried out all the pain and the many other unidentifiable emotions attacking her, Dee was by her side, seated on the edge of the bed and stroking her head in an effort to comfort her.

'Where's Theo?' Billie whispered instantly.

'I put him down for his nap.'

'Sorry about this,' Billie mumbled, sliding off the bed to go into the bathroom and splash her face with cold water because her eyes and her nose were red.

When she reappeared, Dee gave her an uncomfortable look. 'That was *him*, wasn't it? Theo's dad?'

Billie didn't trust herself to speak and she simply nodded.

'He's absolutely gorgeous,' Dee remarked guiltily. 'I'm not surprised you fell for him but what's with the limousine? You said he was well off, not that he was minted...'

'He's minted,' Billie confirmed gruffly. 'Seeing him again was upsetting.'

'What did he want?'

'Something he's not going to get.'

Rejection was the very last thing Gio had anticipated. After assigning two of his security team to watch Billie round the clock and ensure that she did not disappear again, it occurred to him that perhaps there was another man in her life. The idea sent him into such a violent maelstrom of reaction that he couldn't think straight for several rage-charged minutes. For the very first time ever he wondered how Billie had felt when he had told her about Calisto and he groaned out loud. He didn't do complicated with women but Billie was certainly making it that way.

How had he believed it would be when he turned up out of nowhere? he asked himself impatiently. Billie had asked him to leave: he still couldn't *believe* that. She was angry with him: that reality had sunk in. He had married another woman and she was holding that against him but how could she? Gio raked long brown fingers of frustration through the curly black hair he kept close cropped to his skull. She could not possibly have believed that he might marry *her*…could she?

He was the acknowledged head of his family owing to his grandfather's long-term ill health, and it had always been Gio's role and responsibility to rebuild the aristocratic, conservative and hugely wealthy Letsos clan. He had vowed as a boy that he would never repeat the mistakes his own father had made. His great-grandfather had had a mistress, his grandfather had had a mistress but Gio's father had been less conventional. Dmitri Letsos had divorced Gio's mother to marry his mistress in a seriously destructive act of disloyalty to his own blood. Family unity had never recovered from that blow and the older man had forfeited all respect. Gio's mother had died and he and his sisters' childhoods had been wrecked while Dmitri had almost bankrupted the family business in an effort to satisfy his spendthrift second wife's caviar tastes.

Well, if there was another man in Billie's bed, he would soon find out, Gio rationalised with clenched teeth and a jaw line set rock hard with tension. In twenty-four hours he would have the background report from Henley Investigations. Regrettably he was not a patient man and he had assumed she would throw herself back into his arms the instant he told her that he was divorced. Why hadn't she?

Her response when he'd kissed her had been...*hot*. In fact Gio got hard just thinking about it, his libido as much as his brain telling him exactly what and who he needed back in his life. He wondered if he should send her flowers. She was *crazy* about flowers, had always been buying them, arranging them, sniffing them, growing them. It had been selfish of him not to buy her a house with a garden, he conceded darkly, wondering what other oversights he must've made when the woman who had once worshipped the ground he walked on now felt able to show him the door. No woman had *ever* done that to Gio Letsos. He knew he could have virtually any woman he wanted but that wasn't a consolation when he only wanted Billie back where she belonged: in his bed.

After a disturbed night of sleep, Billie rose around dawn, fed all the kids and tidied up. It was only at weekends that she and Dee saw much of each other. On weekdays, she took the kids to school to allow Dee, who worked evenings as a bartender in a local pub, a little longer in bed. Theo went to work with Billie in the mornings and Dee collected him at lunchtime and minded the three kids for the afternoon. After the shop closed, they all ate an early evening meal together before Dee went off to do her shift. It was an arrangement that worked very well for both women and Billie was fond of Dee and her company because her two years in a city apartment where Gio was only an occasional visitor had been full of lonely days and nights.

Of course, in those days she had learned to make good use of her free time, she acknowledged wryly. In those two years with Gio she had acquired GCSEs and two A-levels, not to mention certificates in various courses ranging from cordon-bleu cookery and flower arranging to business start-up qualifications. Gio might not have noticed any of that or have shown the smallest interest in what she did when he wasn't around, but making up for the education she had missed out on while she was acting as her grandmother's carer throughout the teenage years had done much to raise Billie's low self-esteem. After all, when she had first met Gio she had been working as a cleaner because she had lacked the qualifications that would have helped her to aspire to a better-paid job.

As she placed the new pieces of costume jewellery on display in the battered antique armoire she had bought for that purpose, she was a thousand mental miles away on an instinctive walk down the memory lane of her past. Unlike Gio, Billie did not have a proper family tree or at least if she did it was unknown to her. Her mother, Sally, had been an only child, who had reputedly gone wild as a teenager. As Billie's only source of information about her mother had been her mean-spirited grandmother she was inclined to take that story with a pinch of salt. Billie had no memory of ever meeting Sally and absolutely no idea who had fathered her, although she strongly suspected that his name had been Billy.

Billie's grandma and her mother had lived separate lives for years before the day Sally turned up without warning on her parents' doorstep with Billie as a baby. Her grandfather had persuaded her grandmother to allow Sally to stay for one night, a decision she had had Billie's lifetime to loudly and repeatedly regret because when the older woman got up the next morning she had discovered that Sally had gone, leaving her child behind her.

Unfortunately, Billie's grandma had neither wanted nor loved her and, even though she received an allowance from social services for raising her grandchild, her resentment of the responsibility had never faded. Billie's grandpa had been more caring but he had also been a drunk and only occasionally in a fit state to take an interest in her. Indeed, Billie had often thought that her background was the main reason why she had been such a pushover for Gio. His desire for her, his apparent need to look after her, had been the closest thing to love that she had ever known. So, although she would never have admitted it to him, she had been madly, insanely happy with Gio because he had made her *feel* loved…right up until the dreadful day he'd told her that he had to get married and father a child for the sake of his all-important snobby Greek family and his precious business empire.

Chilled by the sobering and humiliating recollection that Gio had not even considered her a possible candidate for a ring, Billie brought out the new garments she had prepared at home and began to price the stock. Theo was napping peacefully in his travel cot in his little cubbyhole at the back of the shop. Customers browsed, purchased and departed as she served them while she worked. Only a month earlier, she had hired her first employee, a Polish woman called Iwona, who did part-time hours when Billie couldn't be at the shop. In fact, the business was doing well and was steadily fulfilling all Billie's hopes. But then she had always loved the character and superior workmanship of vintage clothes and she was careful only to stock quality items. Slowly but surely she had built up a list of regular customers.

Gio climbed out of his limo while his chauffeur argued with the traffic warden and his security team

were disgorged from the vehicle behind. He scanned
the shop front, adorned with the name, 'Billie's Vintage', and frowned, positively transfixed by the idea
that Billie could have opened up her own business.
Yet there was the proof in front of him. *Theos!* He
shook his arrogant dark head, thinking that women
were strange, unpredictable creatures and finally
wondering if he had ever really known Billie at all
because nothing that she had done or said so far had
appeared on his list of her potential reactions. His
frown grew even darker, lending a saturnine quality
to his hard, dark features. He had important projects
to manage and people to see and yet here he was still
stuck after twenty-four exceedingly boring hours in
a back-end-of-nowhere Yorkshire town chasing Billie! What kind of sense did that make?

Dee and Iwona arrived at the shop within minutes
of each other. Dee strapped Theo into his pram and
asked Billie what she fancied eating for supper while
Iwona wrapped a purchase for a customer. That was
when Gio strode in, utterly frying Billie's brain cells
because she stopped mid-conversation with Dee and
totally forgot what she had been about to say.

Garbed in a charcoal designer pinstripe suit that
sheathed his tall, muscular body like a tailor-made
glove, Gio simply took her breath away. His white
shirt accentuated his bronzed complexion and the
very masculine black stubble already beginning to
shadow his handsome jaw line. A startling sunburst of
honeyed heat blossomed between Billie's thighs and
she pressed them tight together, her colour steadily

climbing. She was even more painfully aware of the swelling heaviness of her breasts and the sudden tightening of her nipples. She was appalled that Gio could still have that immediate an effect on her, an effect that was markedly more intense than the day before when she had blamed her surrender to that kiss on the fact that he had caught her unprepared. What was her excuse this time?

'Billie...' Gio breathed in his dark, velvet drawl, poised several feet away and acting as if his appearance in her shop were the most natural thing in the world.

'G-Gio...' she stammered half under her breath, quickly closing the space between them, fearful of being overheard. 'Why are you here?'

'You're not stupid, don't act it,' Gio advised, glancing around. 'So, you left me to open a shop—'

'You. Left. Me,' Billie spelt out with a bitterness she could not restrain but it was the truth: he had left her to place a wedding ring on another woman's finger.

'We can't talk here. We'll catch up back at my hotel over lunch,' Gio decreed, closing a hand round her arm.

'If you don't let go, I'll slap you!' Billie hissed, determined not to be railroaded by his overpowering personality and drive.

His dark eyes glittered like pyrite as if the prospect of a good slap was an entertaining challenge. 'Lunch, *pouli mou*?'

'We've got nothing to say to each other,' Billie told

him, noting that his entire hand was still wrapped round her arm, forcing her to stay by his side.

His sensual mouth quirked as he studied her full pink mouth. 'Then you can *listen*—'

Butterflies danced in her tummy as she looked up at him. 'Don't want to talk, don't want to listen either—'

'Tough,' Gio pronounced and then he did something she would never ever have dreamt he would do in public. He just bent down and scooped her up off her feet and headed for the door.

'Put me down, Gio!' she gasped, making a wild grab at the flouncy skirt of her dress, which had flown up to expose her thighs. 'Have you gone crazy?'

Gio glanced at the two women standing together behind the counter. 'I'm taking Billie out for lunch. She'll be back in a couple of hours,' he explained with complete cool.

'*Gio!*' Billie launched in disbelief, catching a glimpse of Dee's laughing face before Gio shouldered open the door and hid her cousin from view.

The chauffeur swept open the passenger door as if they were royalty and Gio shoved her into the back seat with scant ceremony. 'You should've known that I wouldn't stand there arguing with an audience,' he pointed out smoothly. 'In any case, I'm out of patience and I'm hungry.'

In a series of angry motions, Billie smoothed down her dress, tugging it over her knees. 'Why didn't you go back to London yesterday?'

'You should know by now that saying no to me only makes me try harder.'

Billie rolled her bright green eyes in mockery and said angrily, 'Well, how would I know that when I never did say no to you?'

Disconcertingly Gio laughed, genuine amusement illuminating his darkly handsome face. 'I've missed you, Billie.'

Her annoyance fell away and she turned her head in a sharp movement, both shaken and hurt by that claim and by how very empty it was. 'You got married. How could you possibly have missed me?'

'I don't know but I did,' Gio ground out truthfully. 'You were so much a part of my life.'

'No, I was like one tiny little drawer in a big busy cabinet of drawers,' Billie countered. 'I was never part of the rest of your life.'

Gio was sincerely astonished by that statement. He had phoned her twice a day every day no matter where he was in the world and no matter how busy he was. Her soothing happy-go-lucky chatter had provided him with necessary downtime from a hectic schedule. In truth he had never had so close a relationship with any woman either before or after her. He had trusted her and he had been honest with her, which was a very rare thing between a single man and a single woman in Gio's world. *But* it was steadily sinking in on him that none of that mattered because he had married Calisto. Billie, who had never shown a jealous, distrustful streak in her life, had clearly been jealous and distressed by that development. He didn't like that idea, he didn't like it at all, and he kicked out that thought so fast it might never have existed.

Gio had constructed a protective shell while he was still a child to ensure that he could remain untouched by emotional reactions. Emotion didn't need to get involved. Emotion complicated and only exacerbated an already difficult situation. Calm, common sense and control had always worked far more efficiently for Gio in every field of his life, only *not* with Billie, he acknowledged grudgingly. But the past was the past and he couldn't change it, while life had taught him that with enough money, energy and purpose he could form the future into any shape he wanted.

Billie, however, was not practical; she was all about emotion and perhaps that essential difference between them had been one of the things that attracted him to her and which was now sending her in the wrong direction. His shrewd, dark eyes rested on her angry, flushed face and suddenly he wanted to flatten her to the seat of the limo and teach her that there were far more satisfying responses. Inky spiky lashes lowering, he scanned her from her bright eyes to her lush mouth right down over the glorious breasts he had loved to play with and the long shapely legs he had loved to slide between. Sex with Billie was *amazing*. Just thinking about her made heaviness stir at his groin. Being with her without being able to reach out and take what he wanted, what he had once taken for granted, not only felt weird, but also struck him as a form of refined torture.

'I want you back,' Gio declared with stubborn force. 'I've been looking for you ever since you disappeared.'

'Your wife must've liked that.'

'Leave Calisto out of this…'

Even the sound of her name on Gio's lips stung Billie like a whip across tender skin. She knew she was being too sensitive. He had married another woman two years ago and she needed to move on. Even if *he* hadn't moved on? That was too complex for her, shouted too loudly of wishful thinking. And, my goodness, she had done enough of that while she was still with him and what had those optimistic hopes got her? A broken heart and, right now, the pieces of that foolish heart were rattling like funeral bells. This was the guy she had loved as she had never dreamt she could ever love anyone and he had damaged her beyond forgiveness. Even walking away as she had known she must had almost destroyed her, but not even for him would she have sunk low enough to sleep with another woman's husband.

'I can't believe you're wasting your time with this,' Billie admitted abruptly, her soft full mouth compressed to a flat, tense line. 'I mean, what are you doing here? Why do you even want to see me again? It makes no sense for either of us!'

Gio searched her animated face and wondered what made her seem so beautiful to him. In some corner of his brain, he knew that from a purist's point of view she never had met and never would meet the standard tenets of beauty because her nose turned up at the end and her eyes and her mouth were too big for her face and in a sudden shower of rain her hair turned into an unbelievably frizzy mess. But dry it fell in a silky tangle of curls the colour of toffee half-way to her waist and that hair had cloaked his body many, many times on occasions so intimate it hurt to remember them and still be deprived of the right to repeat them.

'Stop looking at me like that,' Billie told him thinly, the colour of awareness mantling her cheeks, a warm glow unfurling low in her body to remind her of how much time had passed since she had last been touched. She had got pregnant, become a new mother, set up a new home and business and kept so busy-busy-busy for months on end that she fell into bed exhausted every night. It took Gio's reappearance to remind her that life could offer more self-indulgent pastimes.

'Like what?'

'Like we're still…you know,' she completed, eye-lashes lowering.

'Like I still want to be inside you?' Gio queried thickly. 'But I do and right at this very minute I'm aching for you…'

A tiny clenching sensation in a place she refused to think about forced Billie to shift uneasily on the seat. 'I really didn't need to know that, Gio. That was a *very* inappropriate comment to make—'

Gio skated a long forefinger down over the back of the hand she had tautly braced to the leather seat. 'At least it was honest and you're not being honest—'

'I'm not coming back to you!' Billie interrupted loudly. 'I've got another life now—'

'Another man?' Gio slotted in, deep accented voice raw with unspoken vibrations.

And Billie seized on that convenient excuse like a drowning swimmer thrown a lifebelt. 'Yes. There's someone else.'

Every lean, long line of Gio's big body tensed. 'Tell me about him.'

Billie was thinking about her son. 'He's extremely important to me and I would never do anything to hurt or upset him.'

'There's nothing I won't do to get you back,' Gio warned as the limousine drew up outside his country-house hotel and the chauffeur leapt out to open the door. He also grasped at that same moment that he was not as law-abiding as he had always assumed because he knew that he was willing to break rules in order to get Billie back.

Billie stole a reluctant glance at his lean, hard face, clashing with the golden glitter of his stunning eyes. She froze in consternation at that expression of menace she had never seen there before. 'Is there some reason you can't let me be happy without you?' she asked suddenly. 'I think I've paid my dues, Gio.'

Gio's nostrils flared at that declaration, exasperation roughening the edges of an anger he knew he had no right to express. If she had another man, she would naturally get rid of him because he refused to credit that any other man could set her on fire the way he did. But nothing could assuage his bone-deep ferocious reaction to being forced to imagine Billie in bed with someone else. Billie had always been his alone, indisputably *his*.

As they crossed the foyer of the opulent hotel a familiar voice hailed Billie and she stopped dead and flipped round with a smile as a tall blond man in expensive country casuals moved towards her eagerly to greet her.

'Simon, how are you?' she said warmly.

'I've got an address for you.' Simon dug into his wallet to produce a piece of paper. 'Got a pen?'

Billie realised her bag had been left behind at the shop and looked expectantly at Gio. 'Pen?' she pressed.

Totally unaccustomed to being ignored while others went about their business around him, Gio withdrew a gold pen from his pocket with pronounced reluctance, his beautiful obstinate mouth sardonic.

Simon borrowed the pen and wrote the address on the back of a business card. 'There's a heap of stuff there you'll like and it won't cost you much either. The seller just wants the house cleared.'

Impervious to the reality that Gio was standing by her side like a towering and forbidding pillar of black ice, Billie beamed at the taller man. 'Thanks, Simon. I really appreciate this.'

Simon studied her with the same appreciation Gio had often seen on male faces around Billie and his perfect white teeth gritted. 'Maybe you'll let me treat you to lunch here some day soon?'

Gio shot an arm like a statement round Billie's slender spine. 'Regrettably she's already taken.'

Ignoring that intercession, Billie reddened but kept on valiantly smiling. 'I'd like that, Simon. Call me,' she suggested while knowing that she was only encouraging the other man to make a point for Gio's benefit and feeling guilty about that because Gio was making her behave badly as well.

'What was that all about?' Gio demanded grittily as he urged her into the lift.

'Simon's an antique dealer. He tips me off about house clearances. I know a lot of dealers. That's how I built up my business,' Billie advanced with pride.

'You can open a shop in London. I'll pay for it,' Gio told her grimly.

Unimpressed, Billie glanced wryly at him. 'Well, in a roundabout way you paid for this one *and* my house, so I don't think it would be right for you to pay anything more.'

'What are you talking about?'

'I sold a piece of jewellery for cash. It was something you gave me.'

Gio frowned. 'You left everything I ever gave you behind.'

'No, I took one piece. Your very first gift,' Billie extended. 'I had no idea how much it was worth. That was a surprise, I can tell you.'

'Was it?' Gio couldn't even remember his first gift to her and he would have been prepared to swear, having checked the jewellery she left behind, that she had taken nothing with her when she walked out.

'Yes, you're so extravagant it's a wonder you're not broke. You hardly knew me and yet you spent an absolute fortune on that diamond pendant,' Billie told him critically. 'It paid for my house and setting up the shop. I couldn't believe how valuable it was!'

Gio thrust open the door of his suite. And just like that, the memory of the gift returned to him. He had bought the pendant after their first night together and he was furious that she had just sold it as if it meant nothing to her. 'I don't believe that there's another man in your life.'

'I'm not coming back to you,' Billie told him in the most ludicrously apologetic tone. 'Why would I want a shop in London? Why would I want to move? I'm happy here. And believe it or not there are men out there who would take me out with them into a public restaurant instead of hiding me inside their suite!'

Billie had served a direct hit. Gio paled beneath his Mediterranean tan. 'We're in my suite only because we need a private setting in which to talk.'

Billie gave him a wry smile. 'Maybe that's true this one time, Gio, but when it went on for almost two years, even I got the message. You might as well have been married from the moment I met you. I was like a guilty, dirty secret in your life.'

'That is not true.'

'No point arguing about the past now,' Billie parried with determination. 'It's not worth it.'

'Of course it is…I want you back.' A spasm of open exasperation crossed Gio's lean dark face when a knock sounded on the door, announcing the arrival of two waiters pushing a rattling trolley: lunch had arrived.

Billie folded her arms, thinking of her grandpa's favourite winning racehorse, Canaletto, and the reality that just four years ago she had never heard of the artist called Canaletto before. Recalling that blunder still made Billie cringe and die inside herself, for the moment she had entered the conversation she had known her mistake but it had been far too late to cover it up. Unhappily for her, the one and only time Gio had taken her out to mix with his friends she had made an outsize fool of herself...*and* him.

Although he had reacted with neither anger nor criticism, he had dismissed her attempts to talk about the incident and explain that she had grown up more at home in betting shops than museums. But she had known that she had seriously embarrassed him in public in a way that would not be forgotten and, even worse, in a manner that had literally signposted the reality that she and Gio came from worlds and educational backgrounds that were light years apart.

That was why she had never complained about being excluded from his social life and why she had happily settled for dinners out alone in discreet locations where he was unlikely to meet anyone he knew. She had guessed that he was worried she would let him down again and without his awareness she had swiftly set about a self-improvement course in the hope that eventually he would notice and give her another chance. Sadness filled Billie when she recalled that naivety born in the early months of their relationship before she had reached the daunting moment of discovery and slow, painful acceptance that she was *not* Gio's girlfriend but instead his mistress, there to dispense sexual entertainment and not much else and never ever to be taken seriously.

'You're so quiet. I'm not accustomed to you being quiet with me,' Gio confessed in growing frustration, closing his hands over her slender, taut shoulders, massaging the tense muscles there as the door flipped shut behind the waiters. 'Talk to me, Billie. Tell me what you want.'

Feeling the warm tingling of his touch snaking down her rigid spine and the pinching tautness of her nipples while resisting a powerfully seductive urge to lean back into the strong, sheltering heat of Gio, Billie pulled away and quickly sank down into one of the chairs by the beautifully set table. *Talk to me.* That was an insanely perplexing invitation to receive from a male like Gio, who didn't like serious conversations and who smoothly sidestepped or downright ignored emotional moments and phrases.

'We've got nothing to discuss,' she pointed out, tucking into the first course with sudden appetite because while she ate she did not have to speak and had less excuse to be looking at Gio. Gio, surely one of the most beautiful men ever born? She glanced at him from below her lashes, roaming with helpless appreciation across his sculpted features to relish the spectacular slash of his high cheekbones and the tough masculine angle of his jaw. He was out of her reach. He was rich and successful, handsome and sophisticated, educated and pedigreed, everything she was not. He had *always* been out of her reach. If only she had had the wit to accept that obvious fact, she would never have got involved and never have got hurt.

'Is there really another man?' Gio asked very quietly, the rich velvety depth of his accented drawl filling her with pleasure, no matter how hard she tried not to react that way. But that was the same voice she had once lived to hear on the phone when he was away from her, and she could not break her instinctive appreciation.

Billie worked out the question and flushed as she collided with stunning tigerish golden eyes surrounded by ebony lashes. She breathed in, intending to lie, breathed out, knew that for some reason she didn't want to lie. Perhaps it was because if she lied he would come down on her like a granite block to get further information about the supposed man in her life and would eventually cleverly trip her up and learn that she was lying, which would only make her look stupid. 'No, there isn't,' she admitted grudgingly. 'But that doesn't change anything between us.'

'Then we're both free,' Gio murmured lazily, topping up her glass with the bottle of wine.

'I have no intention of getting involved with you again,' Billie declared, taking a hasty gulp of the mellow red, wondering if he would laugh if she told him what the flavour reminded her of. After all, she had once attended a wine course as well as an art-appreciation course and had never had the opportunity to show off what she had learned there.

'But we work well together.'

Billie shook her head in vehement rejection of that statement and concentrated on her food again.

Sipping his wine, Gio watched her. He suspected she was wearing vintage clothes and the pale green linen dress she wore teamed with a light blouse-like jacket embroidered with flowers didn't bear any resemblance to what he deemed to be current fashion, but the colours and plain styling had an understated elegance. The minute she sat down, however, the fabric of the dress pulled taut across the swell of her ample bosom. Gio tensed, hunger stabbing through him while he wondered how he was supposed to tempt a woman so utterly lacking in greed. She didn't want his money, had never wanted his money, had once told him in no uncertain terms that he didn't need a yacht because he would never take the time off to use it. His yacht, sitting idle and costing a fortune to maintain, was currently moored at Southampton.

The waiters came back to serve the main course. She saw their sidewise glances and recognised their curiosity about her. By now the hotel staff would have established who Gio was—Giorgios Letsos, the oil billionaire was a legend the world over. The press loved him because he lived a rich man's life and looked great in print. Calisto had looked brilliant in print too with her sleek straight blonde hair, her perfect features and her terrifyingly tiny size-zero body. Beside her, Billie would have appeared plump, short and ungainly and, from seeing that first photo, Billie had accepted that no comparison could ever be made between them. After all, she and Calisto weren't even on the same page in the looks department.

Gio wound down the tension by talking about his recent travels round the world. She asked small, safe, impersonal questions about some of his staff, a couple of whom she had met and some she had only got to know by speaking to them often on the phone.

While eating her dessert, a glorious concoction of fresh berries and meringue, she enquired whether or not he still had the apartment.

'No…like you, it's long gone,' he stated.

Billie took that to mean that he had not installed a more malleable woman in her place and when a sense of relief filtered through her she gulped more of her wine and tried hard to direct her thoughts to safer topics. It was no longer her business to wonder who he slept with. Once he had married Calisto the question had become academic. Billie had been replaced in every way. Calisto had been chosen to sit at the other end of the dining table in his probably very beautiful Greek home, which Billie had naturally never visited. Gio would have socialised *with* Calisto because they were a real couple and obviously he had planned to make Calisto the mother of his children…

CHAPTER THREE

As the pain of that never-to-be-forgotten reality pierced Billie, she suddenly reached the limits of her tolerance. Her attempt to be civilised for the sake of appearances was shattered and, forced cruelly out of her comfort zone, she thrust her hands down on the edge of the table and suddenly stood up. 'I can't *do* this!' she told Gio with ragged abruptness. 'I want to go home right now!'

Taken aback, Gio sprang upright, a frown line drawing his ebony brows together, his lustrous dark eyes locked to her flushed and unhappy face with wary, searching curiosity. 'What's wrong?'

'Only you would ask that in this set-up!' Billie exclaimed helplessly. 'I didn't want to see you ever again. I don't want to be reminded of the past!'

'Billie...' Gio murmured, closing strong hands over her shaking shoulders while his keen gaze collided with her translucent green eyes. 'Calm down...'

'I can't...I'm not like you...I never was. I'm no good at avoiding the obvious and pretending!' She gasped strickenly, tears clogging up her throat and

terrifying her because in the past she had always contrived to hide her emotional breakdowns from Gio
and she was proud of the restraint she had demonstrated in spite of the provocation and the pain he had
put her through. 'You really shouldn't be here…you
should've left me alone in my new life.'

Gio trailed a blunt forefinger along the lower line
of her lush bottom lip. 'I would if I could. I *had* to
see you again.'

'Why?' Billie demanded baldly.

'Because we weren't done when you walked away.'

A great scream of agonising hurt and frustration was rising up inside Billie. '*Of course* we were
done—you were getting married!' she reminded him
doggedly.

'I had to see you again to find out if I still wanted
you.' Long brown fingers rose to cup her cheekbones.
'And the answer to that is that I *do* still want you.'

In a sudden rage at his nerve in admitting that,
Billie jerked her head back out of reach to detach his
fingers. 'That means nothing.'

'It means a hell of a lot more to me than you seem
to appreciate!' Gio growled, patience splintering, because he was well aware that he was fighting blind in
the sort of emotional confrontation he had absolutely
no experience of dealing with.

'Not enough to make a difference!' Billie snapped
back, a kind of madness in the strong emotions powering her while she fought a humiliatingly defensive
urge to just race out of the door and run away like a
scared kid.

Gio imprisoned her in the strong circle of his arms in an unforewarned movement that jolted her. Brilliant dark eyes blazed pure gold fire down at her. 'There's more than enough for *both* of us,' he spelt out, marvelling that she was still fighting him when it was more normal for him to be fighting off the women who ceaselessly pursued him with flirtation and flattery.

'Let me go!' she told him shakily.

'No.' Gio studied her with smouldering determination. 'You'll only run away again. I can feel it in you and I won't let you do something that stupid again.'

'You can't make me do anything I don't want to—'

'But what about what you *want* to do?' Gio savoured the comeback, bending his handsome dark head to run his tongue along the seam of her closed lips.

Taken by surprise, Billie jerked, her blood running heavily and slowly through her veins as if time itself had slowed down to give her the chance to catch up. His breath fanned her cheek and his lips connected with hers in a heart-stopping collision that tripped her ability to breathe. His lips were smooth and unusually gentle and soft and somehow she couldn't prevent herself from turning up her chin to ask for more of the same.

Gio smiled against her lush mouth, hunger beating through him like a jackhammer. He wanted her more than he had ever wanted anything or anybody in his life and he was all fired up to fight hard for what he wanted because he knew she would restore the oasis

of peace he needed in his private life. Long fingers
smoothed over her back, his other hand curving to
her waist. He nipped at her soft lower lip and then
glided his sensual mouth over hers in a move that
swallowed her tiny cry of surprise. His hand moved
up to tangle in her mane of curls and the pressure of
his mouth increased until her head tilted back, allow-
ing him greater access.

Her breasts crushed against the solid wall of his
broad chest, Billie was struggling to breathe and
being bombarded by sensations she had forced herself
to forget. She had forgotten how gentle he could be
and how inventive and her heartbeat was racing like
an express train because it had been too long since
she had been touched, too long since she had allowed
herself to be the passionate woman that she was.

His tongue darted between her teeth, searching
out the moist welcome beyond and then tasting her
deep and slow with a rough sensuality that lit a string
of firecrackers low in her pelvis. She squirmed as
the heat of his mouth on hers grew and the hunger
she had tried to deny leapt up inside her in explosive
response. The rhythmic plunge of his tongue was
matched by the small rocking motions of his hips
against hers and her body went nuclear on memories
she had suppressed for two years. The barrier of their
clothing could not conceal the fact that Gio was erect
and ready for her.

Billie felt him lift her but she was so drunk on the
taste and texture of his passionate kisses she ignored
the fact. He was more intoxicating than wine and her

head swam while powerful pulses of reaction were coiling up from the tight knot forming at the heart of her body. Her back connected with a soft yielding surface and he lifted his proud, dark head, black cropped hair ruffled by her seeking fingers, burnished dark golden eyes holding hers in an exchange so familiar it shook her to her very depths.

'My tie's choking me,' he confided huskily, yanking at the offending item, ripping loose the collar of his shirt and, in his impatience, sending the button flying.

That comment was typical of Gio: an emotional moment instinctively avoided. When she looked at him, though, everything else melted away for her. It was a desire so all-encompassing it thrummed through Billie like a sensual drugging pulse. He shrugged out of his jacket, used his feet to push off her shoes.

'I can't let you go again, *pouli mou*.'

'You have to...we can't do this,' Billie whispered unevenly, her awareness returning to encompass the giant bed and the elegant furnishings of what was obviously the bedroom of his suite. She was stunned, still dimly wondering how she had got there.

'Open your mouth for me,' Gio urged with stubborn single-minded zeal. '*Theos*, I love your mouth—'

Just one more kiss, she bargained with herself frantically, her body coming alive in the most fatally seductive fashion because with the life came the cravings she had successfully shut down. And he tasted like heaven, a banquet for the starving, a delicious drink for the terminally thirsty. Her hands kneaded his bulging biceps and, brushing aside his collar, she pushed her mouth against the corded strength of his neck, licking the salt from his skin. His big body shifted in a jerk against hers, sealing every line of his muscled mass to hers, and the awesomely familiar weight of him and the scent of his skin plunged her back into the past.

Gio rolled onto his side to drag off her jacket and locate the zip of the dress. He ran it down, stroked it down her arms and fell on the heavenly globes of her full breasts with a hunger he could no more have controlled than he could have stopped breathing.

Billie surfaced from her sensual spell as her bra fell away and Gio cupped her breasts, thumbing the straining strawberry-pink peaks into swollen buds and then using his mouth, the gliding caress of his teeth and the lash of his tongue to stimulate the sensitive nubs beyond bearing. She couldn't stay still. Somewhere in the back of her mind she knew she was going to have regrets but she couldn't listen to them, couldn't detach herself long enough from the scorching urgency of Gio's passion or the staggering strength of her own increasing need.

With a skilled hand he traced the taut triangle of lace stretched between her restive thighs and an inarticulate sound of helpless encouragement broke from her lips. He ravaged her mouth with a wild, devouring kiss and her hips rose, her hands clawing in frustration down the lithe, strong length of his shirt-clad back. Wetness surged to the tender flesh that throbbed. He teased her, stroked her in a sensual torment that drove her to the edge…

'Stop messing about, Gio!' she suddenly gasped in stricken reproach, her body on such a high it was aching and hurting.

Unholy amusement lit up neon signs inside Gio's head and he laughed against her mouth, recalling that she was the only woman who had ever made him laugh in bed. She was also most probably the only woman who could reduce him to the juvenile level of having sex with half his clothes still on. He blanked the thought, the barometer of his mood suddenly darkening, lean, strong face shadowing, but it was no use because he wasn't in control at that moment, didn't even want to be in control, simply craved the hot, wet oblivion of burying himself in her as deeply as possible.

Billie arched up and suddenly he was there, nudging against her indescribably sensitive entrance before driving his long, hard thickness into her tight channel. She cried out, flung her head back and her back arched as she convulsed around him, her cries of helpless pleasure filling the air as he angled back from her and plunged again with dominant force. The hot excitement of his every virile thrust consumed her, sending out eddying ripples of ever-growing pleasure from her womb. The pace became fast and frantic and the friction of his powerful rhythm stimulated her response to an unbearable height, and she bucked before he sent her flying into another powerful climax, ecstasy flooding every inch of her body.

Within seconds of satiation, Gio turned cold, pushing off the bed and grabbing what little clothing he had removed to head for the bathroom. He was outraged and downright unnerved by the sheer intensity of his own need. Without a doubt, Billie was special, terrific in bed but nothing more, nothing greater, for nobody knew better than Gio Letsos that any form of attachment endangered a man's power and control. He could keep his hands off her if he had to; *obviously* he could exist perfectly well without her. Billie was an indulgence, not a necessity.

As he ripped off what remained of his clothes he rested his hot, damp forehead against the cold tiled wall for several tense seconds, hands coiled into tight fists of angry restraint. For an instant images from the worst day of his life reclaimed him and he broke out into a cold sweat, his quick and clever brain reacting accordingly. Wanting or needing a woman too much was weak and foolish; enjoying good sex was normal: he had just enjoyed very, *very* good sex.

CHAPTER FOUR

LIKE AN ACCIDENT VICTIM, Billie sat up in the tangled and creased remnants of her clothes. She blinked and then the realisation of what had just happened kicked in and she hated herself with a virulence that literally hurt. In shock, she struggled to deal with a colossal self-betrayal. Gio would never believe she wanted to be left alone now, would he? Not when she glugged down a couple of glasses of wine over lunch with him as if they were old and dear friends and then got upset and *still* went to bed with him!

How could I have? Theo's trusting little face below his mop of black curls swam inside her head. What had happened to her self-respect? She had wanted Gio with a desperate hunger that in retrospect shook her inside out. Had she missed sex that much? She fought her way into her knickers with clumsy, trembling hands. The bathroom door opened and she froze before sliding off the bed, gathering up her discarded clothing, locked in a cocoon of almost-sick mortification.

'I didn't plan for this to happen…' Gio breathed curtly.

Engaged in getting her bra back on, it was as much as Billie could do to even spare a glance in his direction. She was surprised that he wasn't sporting a triumphant smile because he had won and Gio liked to win much more than most people. It was the high-voltage combination of that essential drive, innate aggression and competitiveness that made Gio Letsos a global success.

'Like I believe that,' Billie framed dully while she slid into her dress because she knew how intensely manipulative and devious he could be. He used those qualities in business. She was quite sure he had used them on her and was still doing so. Conscience didn't get much of a look-in with Gio when it came to anything he wanted.

'Let me...' He strode round the foot of the bed to run up her zip and she wanted to slap his hands away and scream, only that would have humiliated her even more by exposing just how much he had wounded her. 'I didn't plan it,' he repeated.

'Right, you didn't plan it,' Billie echoed like a well-taught parrot, pushing her feet into her shoes, wanting a shower badly but desperate to escape his presence and reach the sanctuary of her home and her son.

'Next week you have your twenty-fifth birthday,' Gio told her.

Billie grimaced. 'My twenty-third—'

Gio looked back at her in bewilderment. 'Twenty-fifth—'

'I lied when we first met,' Billie volunteered carelessly. 'You said you didn't date teenagers and I was nineteen, so I said I was two years older.'

Taken aback, Gio stared at her. 'You *lied*? You were only nineteen?'

Billie nodded and shrugged. 'What does it matter now?'

Biting back a sharp retort, Gio compressed his handsome mouth, his absolute trust in her taking a severe hit because right from the start of their acquaintance he had been disarmed by her apparent honesty. Aside of that he was less than pleased that he had taken a teenager to his bed without even realising it. It had been a much more unequal relationship than he had ever appreciated, he recognised grudgingly. He had been twenty-six years old and about a thousand years of sexual savoir faire and sophistication ahead of her.

'Call me a taxi,' she prompted in the strained silence. 'I want to go home.'

'We haven't agreed anything yet—'

'And we're not going to,' Billie interposed. 'What just happened was an accident, a mistake…a case of familiarity breeding contempt, whatever you choose to call it. But it didn't mean anything to either of us and it didn't change anything…'

Billie waited for Gio to protest but the silence stretched and she was suddenly wretchedly, unhappily aware of how much that silence of agreement hurt. He had travelled from hot-pursuit mode to apparent indifference: it seemed the sex had acted like a miracle cure. And why was she surprised? She had always been surprised that Gio stayed interested in her. She had been surprised throughout their relationship, had never contrived to work out what he saw in her that he could not find in a more beautiful and glossier woman.

'The limo will drop you back,' Gio breathed flatly, his spectacular eyes veiled. 'I have work to catch up on. My business team are joining me here within the hour. I'll call you tomorrow.'

Shot from the conviction that she was being rejected to the news that once again she had read him wrong, Billie slowly shook her head. 'There's no point. End it here, Gio. Leave me alone. You go your way, I go mine. It's the only sensible option after all this time.'

A sliver of dark fury shot through Gio that Billie should still feel detached enough to believe that she could easily walk away from him. This was the woman he had once believed *loved* him. This was the woman he had spent a fortune tracking down. Well, so much for love, he reflected without wonder at that change in her and her lack of appreciation for a persistent and flattering pursuit that many women would have killed to receive from him. Was his less-than-stellar performance between the sheets at fault? Shorn of his usual cool, he had been too fast and too eager. His perfect white teeth gritted.

'You're starting to offend me,' Gio admitted with the disconcerting honesty he could occasionally employ to unsettle the opposition. He tugged out his phone and voiced terse instructions in Greek. 'Perhaps it's better that you leave now and think over what you're doing.'

Billie flushed, hands linking tightly in front of her. 'I've already thought—'

'If I leave, I never come back,' Gio spelt out in pure challenge. 'Think carefully before I give you what you say you want.'

A pang of dismay shot through Billie. She wanted him to go away and leave her alone, of course she did. She didn't have a single doubt. She had to protect Theo because Gio would hit the roof if he found out about him. His Greek family was very traditional and old-fashioned and children born on the proverbial wrong side of the blanket were not welcomed. She knew his father had had an illegitimate child with a lover, a half-sister of Gio's, whom his family did not acknowledge or accept into their select circle.

Gio was finally coming round to her arguments, she decided, striving to feel pleased that her objections were finally getting through to him and being taken seriously. But just then, as Gio showed her back out to the lift and turned away again without a backward glance to vanish into his suite, it was impossible for Billie to feel good about anything that had happened. She was a mess inside and out and she hadn't even brushed her hair. The mirrored wall in the lift showed a woman with a reddened swollen mouth, a wild torrent of tousled curls and guilty troubled eyes gritty with the tears she was denying. Did she blame the wine? Being sex-starved? Old memories and familiarity? Or did she have a fatal weakness called Gio Letsos? And without any warning, time was sweeping her boldly back to their very first meeting.

Billie's grandfather had died when she was eleven. Seven years later, her grandma had passed away after a very long illness. The older woman had willed her house to a local charity and had essentially left Billie homeless. Billie had travelled down to London with another girl, moved into a hostel and found work as a cleaner in a luxury block of apartments. She had cleaned Gio's palatial apartment daily for several months before she met him.

Before she'd entered any apartment she had rung the bell to check whether anyone was at home and there had been no answer that day. Billie had been dusting shelves in the vast open-plan living area when a sudden unexpected noise had made her jump in fright. Whirling round, she had belatedly realised that there was a man lying slumped on one of the sofas. For an instant she had believed he was asleep, but his dark golden brown eyes had opened to stare at her and he had immediately begun trying to sit up, his movements clumsy and uncoordinated. She had watched in shock as, instead of standing, he had ended up rolling off the sofa and falling heavily to the polished wooden floor.

'For goodness' sake…are you all right?' she had exclaimed, wondering if he was in a drunken stupor.

But having grown up with a grandfather and school friends who liked to overindulge in alcohol at every opportunity, Billie had trusted her ability to recognise when someone was drunk. Gio had tried and failed to lift his head and he had groaned. She had noted that there was no sign of a bottle or a glass anywhere and no smell of drink before she had finally risked moving closer to see if he was simply ill.

'Flu…' he had mumbled, ridiculously long black lashes dropping back down over his stunning eyes as if even the effort of speech was too much for him.

Billie had rested cool fingers fleetingly on his forehead and registered that he was running one heck of a fever. 'I think you need an ambulance,' she had whispered.

'No…doctor…phone,' he had framed with difficulty, patting the pocket of his business suit jacket.

Billie had dug out the phone for him and slotted it into his hand. He had fumbled with buttons and cursed. 'No, you do it.'

But the contacts list had been written in some weird script that was definitely not the alphabet and most probably a foreign equivalent. She had had to shake his shoulder to bring that to his attention and with some difficulty at focusing he had stabbed out the name for her and she had had to make the call to the doctor for him. Mercifully the doctor had spoken English and, sounding very concerned about the male he'd referred to as 'Gio', he had promised to be with them in twenty minutes.

Feeling uncomfortable but knowing she had to wait to let the doctor into the apartment, Billie had got on with the cleaning while Gio had lain there on the floor. She had felt helpless and useless because he was simply too big and heavy in build for her to lift him in an effort to make him more comfortable. The doctor, young and fit, had been shocked to see

Gio lying on the floor and had immediately hauled him up and practically carried him into the first bedroom off the corridor.

Ten minutes later, the doctor had sought her out in the kitchen. 'He's a workaholic and he's exhausted, which is probably why he's ill. It's a bad dose of the flu and he won't go to hospital. I'll bring back his prescription and look into getting a private nurse…in the short term, can you stay for a while? He shouldn't be alone but I'm on emergency call—'

'I'm only here to clean and I'm already behind,' Billie had explained apologetically. 'I should be starting on the apartment next door—'

'Gio owns the building. He's probably the man who signs your pay cheque through the management company. I wouldn't worry about the place next door,' the doctor had told her drily. 'He asked for you to go in and see him—'

'But why?'

The doctor had shrugged on his way out. 'Maybe he wants to thank you for being a good Samaritan. You could've run and left him lying there.'

She had knocked on the bedroom door and when it wasn't answered had peeped in, seeing Gio sprawled naked but for a pair of black silk pyjama trousers on the biggest bed she had ever seen. Even ill, pale below his olive skin and fast asleep, he had been the most beautiful specimen of masculinity she had ever seen, from his ruffled black curly hair to his unshaven chin and his incredibly impressive bronzed and muscular torso and flat stomach.

She had cleaned the guest bathrooms, waited an hour and then gone back into the bedroom, finding him awake.

'Do you need anything?'

'Water would be welcome...what's your name?' he had asked limply, breathing heavily as he'd tried to sit up but had lurched sideways instead.

'Billie.'

'Short for?'

'Billie. Do you want me to fix your pillows?'

And she had fixed the pillows and straightened the sheet and fetched him a glass of water. He had seemed stunned by the discovery that she cleaned his apartment regularly sight unseen.

'There's never much to do here,' she had admitted. 'You don't seem to use the kitchen.'

'I travel a lot, eat out or order in when I'm here.'

The bell had buzzed. 'That'll be the nurse the doctor mentioned,' she remarked.

'I don't need a nurse.'

'You're too weak and sick to be left alone,' Billie had informed him bluntly.

'I was hoping you'd hang around...'

'I have other apartments to cleanI'll be working late tonight as it is,' she had said before she hurried to answer the door to a beautiful uniformed blonde with the face of a madonna.

The next morning when she had clocked in, her manager had emerged from his office to say, 'You've been seconded full-time to Mr Letsos' apartment until further notice.'

'But how…why on earth? *Full-time?*' she had queried in astonishment.

'The order came down from higher up. Maybe the guy had a party last night and needs the place gutted,' he had muttered without interest. 'It's not our business to question why.'

She had used the bell but nobody had answered and she had let herself in with her pass key, moving quietly round the silent apartment before knocking on the bedroom door.

'Where's the nurse?' she had asked straight away.

Even more badly in need of a shave and still flat on the pillows, Gio had given her a wry look. 'She tried to get into bed with me… I told her to leave.'

Thoroughly disconcerted by that bald admission, Billie had surveyed him wide-eyed, recognising the level of his primal male attraction even in sickness. He was gorgeous. Just looking at him had made butterflies take flight in her tummy.

'For that reason, I hope you don't mind that I arranged for you to take care of me because you haven't demonstrated any desire to get into bed with me—'

Billie had reddened to the roots of her hair. 'Of course not…how did you arrange it?'

'Do you mind?'

'What would taking care of you entail?' Billie had prompted suspiciously. 'I'm no nurse—'

'I haven't eaten since breakfast yesterday,' Gio had confided, stunning lustrous dark eyes locking onto hers in clear search of sympathy. 'Food would be very welcome.'

She had felt sorry for him, had even contrived to feel guilty that she hadn't offered him a meal the day before. And after all, taking care of the sick was pretty much all Billie had done from the age of eleven right up until her grandmother had passed away. For the following three days, Billie had done what came naturally without fuss or fanfare. She had looked after Gio, shopping for him, cooking meals, changing the bed, passing out his medication and arguing with him every time he prematurely announced that he was well enough to get out of bed because his state of exhaustion was still etched in his pallor and sunken eyes. Indeed she had established an amazingly easy camaraderie with Gio Letsos that took no note whatsoever of their divergent status in life and she had laughed out loud when he had announced that he would take her out to dinner as a thank you as soon as he was stronger.

'What age are you?' he had suddenly demanded, staring at her. 'I don't date teenagers.'

And the minute that Billie had appreciated that the dinner suggestion could actually be described as a date, she had lied without shame to fulfil the conditions of acceptance because *any* kind of a date with a male like Gio had struck her as a dream come true.

As the images of the past receded, Billie swallowed hard, shaken up by those recollections and her own innocence, for in those days she had very definitely viewed Gio as a knight on a white horse. He had seemed so perfect to her, so very considerate and courteous. Well, she conceded painfully, she knew how well that belief had turned out... Gio could say the most dreadful things in the politest way without even raising his voice. He could graciously open the door for you while saying something that flayed the skin from your bones and ripped your heart to shreds. His superb manners and self-control had only added another layer of pain to the end game because he was clever enough to voice intolerable expectations in an acceptable, seemingly civilised way.

That same day the head of Gio's security, Damon Kitzakis, came to see him after dinner. Wearing a rare air of discomfiture for a man who was generally very relaxed with his employer, Damon hovered and took his time about speaking up.

'Something worrying you?' Gio encouraged with a frown.

'As you instructed, Stavros has been keeping an eye on Miss Smith and in the course of doing that he got chatting to one of her neighbours,' Damon volunteered stiffly. 'Quite accidentally he picked up something you probably already know about...of course, *but—*'

Gio was steadily becoming very still behind the desk, his broad shoulders taut. 'What is this something?'

'Miss Smith has a child.'

Gio shot him a startled look. 'The woman she lives with has kids.'

Damon winced. 'Apparently when...Miss Smith

moved in when she was pregnant. The youngest kid…
the baby…is hers.'

Suddenly something was buzzing in Gio's head,
interfering with his ability to think clearly. He blinked
rapidly, fighting to clear his thoughts. Billie had a
baby, another man's child. There *had* been another
man. *Theos,* he should never have approached her in
advance of seeing the background report he had yet
to receive from Henley. This was his reward for his
ridiculous impatience, he reflected grimly. The least
she could have done was *tell* him, he thought then
with the dull, unfeeling anger of shock.

Pallor framed his mouth as he compressed his lips
hard and phoned Joe Henley. Yes, there was a child,
the older man confirmed without hesitation, but he
hadn't yet got hold of a copy of the birth certificate
and couldn't offer any further details until he did.

Why the hell hadn't Billie just told him that she
was a mother? After all, she had had the perfect
excuse for not resuming their relationship, so why
hadn't she used it? Surely she would have guessed
that he would no longer want her with a kid in tow?
Gio sprang upright. His anger, cold from sheer
shock, was heading towards sizzling temperatures
very fast indeed because Billie had achieved a feat
few people lived to boast about: she had made Gio
feel foolish. He would never have gone to bed with
her again had he known she had a child. Was Billie
playing some silly waiting game, planning to entrap
him with the lure of sex before admitting that she
now had a kid?

* * *

Billie sank into a deep bath and whisked her fingers through the bubbles coating the surface of the water. It was treat night, when she spoiled herself with her favourite things. The children were in bed fast asleep. The kitchen was clean. She would curl up on the sofa and watch a romantic movie and have some chocolate. Even if she no longer quite believed in true love or the staying power of romance she could still enjoy the fantasy, she acknowledged ruefully.

The doorbell went when she was drying herself. And she grimaced, hurriedly reaching for her robe and tying the sash tight round her waist as she sped barefoot down the stairs, keen to prevent her caller from pressing the bell again and disturbing the children. Jade was a light sleeper and once she was up she would be up and there would be no prospect of peace and tranquillity. No, then it would be cartoons and endless chatter until Jade got sleepy again.

Billie yanked open the door and stiffened in dismay. It was Gio, shorn of his usual business suit, wearing black jeans and a leather jacket. She dragged her attention from the rare sight of him in casual clothing up to his lean, hard-boned face. Dark eyes glittered like golden fireworks at her and colour surged up in a hot wave over her cheeks because all she could think about at that instant was the thrusting potency of him over and in her and the earth-shattering pleasure that had followed.

'Why didn't you tell me you had a child?' Gio demanded in a raw undertone.

Billie jerked and lost colour even faster than she had gained it at the recollection of how they had spent the afternoon. She pushed the door wider, immediately recognising that this was not a conversation she could keep outdoors. 'You'd better come in.'

'You're damned right I'm coming in,' Gio all but snarled at her, striding past her and thrusting open the sitting-room door with all the annoying assurance of a regular and more welcome visitor.

He knew. Oh, dear heaven, he knew, and that was why he was furious, Billie assumed in consternation.

Gio swung round from the window, all fluid grace and driving aggression, stunning eyes blistering over her as if she had deeply offended him in some way. 'I'd never have touched you if I'd known you'd had some other man's child!'

Some other man's child. The worst of the tension holding Billie uncannily still evaporated as she realised that by some mysterious good fortune her secret was still a secret. Evidently it had not even occurred to Gio that her child might be his, but she was disconcerted by the unexpected flash of sexual possessiveness he was revealing. 'Yes, I have a child,' she confirmed flatly. 'But I don't see that as your business—'

'*Theos*… Of course it was *my* business when I was asking you to come back to me!' he flung back at her, his spectacular bone structure rigid with condemnation.

So, he didn't want her with the encumbrance of a child. That was no surprise to Billie. He might have wanted a legitimate heir from Calisto but that want had been firmly rooted in his pride in his family line and his apparent desire to have a child to inherit his business empire. He had no particular fondness for children or interest in them that she had ever noticed. He had nephews and nieces because at least two of his sisters had married and produced but he had never mentioned those kids in a positive way, choosing instead to complain about the noise, inconvenience and indiscipline they displayed at adult gatherings.

'But I didn't *owe* you the information that I had a child when I had no plans to come back to you,' Billie countered evenly, slight shoulders setting straight now that she no longer felt threatened, green eyes bright with defiance.

'Then what was this afternoon all about?' Gio demanded with cutting derision.

'A mistake, as I said earlier,' she reminded him doggedly. 'A mistake we will obviously never repeat.'

Gio studied Billie, all pink and tousled and undoubtedly naked below the robe. As she moved her breasts swayed, pointed nubs making faint indents on the fabric, and within seconds he was hard as iron and furious that the hunger he had so recently assuaged could return without his volition. 'Who was the guy?'

'That's not relevant,' Billie fielded.

The fury still powering Gio wouldn't quit. He breathed in slow and deep, disturbed by the level of anger still burning through him, questioning its source. 'What age is the kid?' he asked, although he didn't know why he was asking because he could see no reason why he should want to know.

'A year old,' Billie answered, trimming a couple of months from Theo's tally for safety's sake, fearful of rousing Gio's curiosity and making him wonder if there was the smallest possibility that her child might also be *his* child.

Involved in fast mental calculations as he counted the months, Gio compressed his wide sensual mouth into a hard line of distaste. 'So, it was some kind of rebound thing after me,' he assumed.

'Not everything in my life is about you!' Billie snapped back defensively.

'But obviously the kid's father isn't still around—'

'Not all men are cut out to be fathers,' she parried.

'The least a man should do is stand by his own child,' Gio pronounced, startling her with that opinion. 'It's his most basic duty.'

'Well, mine didn't…' and she almost reminded him that his father hadn't either but that felt like too sensitive a point to raise in the mood he was in.

'Whatever.' Gio shifted a broad shoulder sheathed in butter-soft leather in a Mediterranean shrug as he moved past her to the door, clearly eager to be gone this time around. 'You should've told me about the child the minute I reappeared. It's a game changer, not something I could accept.'

Once, Billie would have assumed that she would experience a certain bitter satisfaction from Gio, in his ignorance, rejecting his own child, but instead guilt bit deep into her uneasy conscience. The passage of time had softened her outlook. Nothing was as black and white as she had believed when she had given birth to Theo without Gio's knowledge. Less emotional now than she had been then, she knew that Gio had wronged her but that Gio's wrong did not necessarily make her decisions right. A child wasn't a trophy or a payback for an adult's unkindness. A child was only a small human being, who might well not appreciate the choice she had made when he was old enough to have an opinion.

For Gio the next morning started with a bang when the fax spewed out a document and kept on printing. He scooped up the first page on the way to the shower and froze when he realised that he was looking at a facsimile of a birth certificate.

Theon Giorgios, a little boy aged fifteen months, had been born to Billie Smith. Theon was his grandfather's name and the child's age left no doubt of when conception had occurred.

Gio swept up the other pages of the report that had come through. His hands were trembling with rage. He was so angry, so incredulous that he wanted to smash something. He had trusted Billie and yet self-evidently she had *betrayed* his trust. He struggled to cool down for long enough to take a rational appraisal of the facts. No method of birth control was fool proof. He knew that intellectually, but he had always been careful, determined never to be caught in that net by something as basic as biology.

Billie had been on the contraceptive pill but side

effects had led to her trying several brands before finally choosing to have an implant put in her arm instead. In short he had allowed her to take contraceptive responsibility and it was very possible that she had simply fallen victim to the failure rate. He set down the report, strode into the shower and, below the pounding beat of the overhead power shower, he thought with an incredulous wonder that was entirely new to his experience, *I have a son.*

An illegitimate son. He didn't like that; he didn't like that aspect at all. Gio was rigid in his views in that line and was well aware that his half-sister had suffered from having neither a father nor the acceptance and support of her own family. Times had changed since then and the world in general was much less concerned about whether or not children were born within marriage. In the Letsos family, however, such formal acknowledgements of inheritance, status and honour still mattered a great deal.

That Billie had lied outright to him shocked Gio the most and by the time he had finished reading that report and had learned about his son's surgery, Billie's unacceptable childcare arrangements and the unsavoury character of the woman she was living with, he wasted no time in setting up a video-conference meeting with his legal team in London to get advice. That discussion concluded, Gio knew what his options were and they were very few and the fierce temper he usually kept under wraps was boiling up like lava below his calm surface. He was in a situation he would never have chosen and, worst of all, a situation he could not necessarily control. He would fight dirty if he had to, *very* dirty if need be. Billie might have taken him by surprise but Gio knew where his priorities lay.

That same morning, Billie felt washed out because she had tossed and turned through the night and she got up early and was sitting with a cup of tea when Dee came downstairs smothering a yawn and swearing she was going straight back to bed.

'I've done something awful,' she confided to her cousin, quickly filling in the details and wincing when Dee looked at her in surprise and dismay. 'I know, it was totally wrong of me to tell Gio that Theo was another man's child—'

'What came over you?'

Billie groaned. 'I felt cornered and threatened. I didn't get the chance to think anything through. I know Gio's going to be furious when he finds out the truth.' She pushed away the curls flopping on her brow and groaned. 'I'm going to text him and ask him to come over.'

'I think you'd better. I mean…the minute you realised that he knew you had a child, you should've come clean. After all, if you don't tell Gio, what happens if Theo decides that he wants to meet his father ten or fifteen years from now?' the blonde woman asked anxiously. 'I know Gio hurt you but that doesn't mean that he couldn't be a good father.'

Dee wasn't telling Billie anything she hadn't thought herself during the long lonely hours of the night. Gio walking back into her life had changed everything. It was no longer acceptable to conceal the truth of Theo's paternity and pretending that some other man was responsible for his conception had been downright unforgivable, she acknowledged with eyes that ached from the tears she was holding back. Ashamed of that moment of cowardice, she swallowed hard and lifted her phone, selecting the number she had never deleted, hoping it remained unchanged, texting...

I have to speak to you today. It's very important.

Gio texted back.

Eleven, your house.

Clearly, Billie was planning to tell him the truth. Gio's mouth curled; he wasn't impressed. The truth would still be coming fifteen months and more too late...

CHAPTER FIVE

RESTIVE AS A cat on hot bricks, Billie peered out of the window as Gio sprang out of the limo and she tensed up even more at the sight of his formal attire. He wore a faultlessly tailored black business suit teamed with a white shirt and purple tie. This was Gio in full tycoon mode, eyes veiled, lean, strong face taut with reserve, and unsmiling.

'I have something to tell you,' she said breathlessly in the hall.

Gio withdrew a folded sheet of paper from his jacket and simply extended it. 'I already know…'

Her heart beating very fast, Billie shook open the sheet, lashes fluttering in disconcertion when she saw the photocopy of the birth certificate. 'I don't know what to say—'

'There's nothing you can say,' Gio pronounced icily. 'You lied last night. You deliberately concealed the truth from me for well over a year. Evidently you had no intention of *ever* telling me that I was a father.'

'I never expected to see you again,' Billie muttered weakly.

'I want to see him,' Gio breathed in a driven undertone.

'He's having a nap—'

Poised at the foot of the stairs, Gio sent her a sardonic appraisal. 'I will still see him…'

Billie breathed in deep and started up the stairs, brushing damp palms down over her jeans. If she was reasonable, even a touch conciliating, they could deal with this situation in a perfectly civilised fashion, she told herself soothingly. Naturally, Gio's first reaction was curiosity and, since he was divorced, Theo's existence was probably less of an embarrassment than it might otherwise have been.

'We need to be quiet,' she whispered. 'Dee's very tired and she went back to bed. I don't want to wake her.'

Billie pressed open the door of the room that the three children shared. Theo's cot was in the corner. Gio strode up to the rails and gazed down with a powerful sense of disbelief at the baby peacefully sleeping in a tangle of covers. *His son.* Even at first glance, the family resemblance was staggering. Theo had a shock of black curls, a strong little nose and the set of his eyes was the same as Gio's. Gio breathed in deep and slow, his broad chest tightening on a surge of emotion unlike anything he had ever felt. This was *his* little boy and he had gone through serious surgery *without* Gio. Any sort of surgery on babies was risky. His child could have died without Gio ever having known of his existence. Rage shot through Gio like a rejuvenating drug, ripping through the carapace of uncertainty and shock. Not trusting himself to remain quiet, he swung away from the cot and walked back to the door.

Billie studied him uneasily. Colour scored along the high blades of his cheekbones. His eyes were a glossy brilliant black she couldn't read and his wide sensual mouth was clenched into a hard line.

'*Theos*...I will never ever forgive you for this,' Gio ground out at the top of the stairs, his dark velvety drawl as chilling as an icicle shot into her flesh.

Consternation winging through her at that inflexible assurance, Billie's tummy flipped and her legs felt hollow and clumsy as she descended the stairs.

In the sitting room she turned round to face him. 'Why won't you forgive me?' she prompted. 'Because I got pregnant?'

A tall, dark, brooding figure in the doorway, Gio stared across the room at her. 'I'm not that stupid. It takes two people to make a baby. I know you couldn't have schemed behind my back to have him because if that had been the case your goal would have been to claim child support. As you made no attempt to contact me to tell me that you had had my child, I can, at least, absolve you of a motive of greed.'

'Am I supposed to say thank you for that vote of confidence?' Billie asked with raised brows.

'No.' Gio closed the door behind him. 'You're supposed to explain why you chose not to tell me.'

'I'm surprised you can ask me that.'

'Are you really?' Gio prompted in a gritty undertone.

'Yes...you were getting married,' Billie pointed out flatly.

'That's not an excuse,' Gio declared harshly. 'Whether I was single, married or divorced that child upstairs was my business and will *always* be my business and that's why you should have told me the minute you realised that you were pregnant.'

'I didn't think you'd want to know,' Billie admitted uncomfortably, wondering exactly what he expected her to say. 'You once warned me that if I got pregnant it would be a disaster and the end of our relationship.'

'That's not an excuse either, particularly as, according to you, our relationship was already at an end,' Gio reminded her staunchly.

'Gio, you know you would've been furious and that you probably would've blamed me for it. I *knew* you wouldn't want me to have your child!' she exclaimed in frustration, resenting his refusal to acknowledge the limits of their relationship at the time.

'What you want and what you get in life are often two very different things,' Gio pointed out cynically. 'I'm adult enough to accept that reality.'

'Oh, thanks a bundle!' Billie snapped back at him, her face flaming. 'How dare you sneer at me because I have your child? I believed that if I'd told you back then, you would have asked me to have a termination—'

Gio shot her a chilling appraisal. 'On what grounds do you base that assumption?'

Aware of the rise of hostile vibrations in the atmosphere, Billie fumbled to find the right words. 'Well, obviously—'

An ebony brow lifted. 'Did I ever make any comment about expecting you to have a termination if the situation arose?'

Put so unerringly on the spot, Billie shifted her feet uneasily. 'Well, no, but once you had admitted what your attitude would be to an unplanned pregnancy it was a natural assumption for me to make.'

'I don't think so.'

'So, you're saying that you wouldn't have suggested a termination?' Billie prompted.

'That's exactly what I'm saying. And considering that we only once briefly discussed how I would feel about you getting pregnant, you made one hell of a lot of assumptions about how I would react to having a child!' Gio condemned.

'At the time you were getting married to *have* a child with another woman. My being pregnant was nothing but bad news on every level!' Billie proclaimed emotively. 'And maybe I didn't care to be the bearer of such bad news, maybe I didn't want to tell you what I knew you didn't want to hear, maybe, just maybe, I had a little pride of my own...'

'I would never have married Calisto had I known you were pregnant,' Gio declared grimly. 'I would always have put the needs of my child first.'

Billie was rocked by that blunt announcement and she frowned. 'I don't understand.'

Gio was beginning to grasp that reality for himself and his temper was on a hair trigger. 'No, you don't understand what you've done,' he told her flatly. 'Do you?'

'What have I done?' Billie fired back defensively. 'I brought Theo into the world and I've looked after him ever since to the best of my ability. He has everything that he needs—'

Gio's eyes flared golden as luminous torches, the force of his anger obvious in the harsh angular lines stamped on his darkly handsome features. 'No, he has not. He has no father—'

Her brow furrowed. 'If you want to play a part in Theo's life, I'll support that…if that's what you're worrying about—'

'You think it's acceptable to offer me a part?' Gio derided in a tone that cracked like a whiplash in the silence. 'You think it's acceptable to let my son go through surgery without even telling me? To raise him here in a dump? To drag him to a shop while you work? To keep him ignorant of my language, his heritage, his father's family, when you don't even have a family of your own to offer him? Let me tell you now that *nothing* you have done is acceptable to me!'

Shaken by that comprehensive denunciation of what she had to offer her child and the fury he couldn't hide, Billie backed off a step. 'My home is not a dump—'

'It *is* on my terms,' Gio fired back unapologetically.

'How did you know that Theo had to have surgery?' Billie asked, thrown by Gio's attitude, which was the exact opposite of what she had expected, and then finally making the leap to guess the most likely source of his information. 'Oh, you've had us investigated, haven't you?'

'Why was my son over six months old before he received surgery?' Gio demanded. 'Hip dysplasia is usually recognised early.'

'His wasn't and when it was other treatments were tried first. You seem to know something about it—'

'Of course I do—there's a genetic link to the condition in my family. My half-sister and one of my full sisters were born with it as well as one nephew and one niece. It's less common in boys. Theo having suffered it was almost as good as a DNA test,' Gio spelt out with sardonic bite. 'He is a Letsos in all but name—'

Billie lifted her chin. 'No, he's a Smith.'

Ramping down his anger, Gio looked at her, lustrous dark golden eyes semi-veiled by the thickness of his lashes. Even dressed in old jeans and a blue cotton top, her lush feminine curves sang a siren's song to him. He hardened, knowing that, no matter how angry he was with her, he still wanted her on the most visceral level. Once had not been enough; once had not sated him. 'I want my son,' he said simply.

Billie turned pale, eyes flickering uncertainly over his lean, tight face, skimming uneasily over the lithe, lethal power of his very well-built body. 'What's that supposed to mean?'

'It means exactly what I said—I *want* my son. I want to be there for him as my father was not there for me,' Gio extended curtly, wide sensual mouth compressing on the grudging admission, reminding her that his background and his family had always been a thorny topic on which he was only prepared to offer the barest details.

'And how do you propose to do that?'

'By fighting you for custody,' Gio countered, throwing his big shoulders back, standing tall. 'My son deserves no less from me.'

Her brow furrowed, consternation and disbelief running through her in a debilitating wave as she collided with his fiery gaze. That visual connection seemed to make the very blood in her veins move sluggishly even while her heartbeat quickened. In turmoil, she shivered. 'You can't be serious. You can't mean that you would try to take Theo away from me?'

'I will not allow him to stay here.'

Anger powered by a deep sense of fear smashed through the wall of Billie's astonishment. 'It doesn't matter what you allow. I'm Theo's mother and what you have to say has nothing to do with it!'

'You're wrong,' Gio told her succinctly. 'I have every right to object to the manner in which you care for my son and I will be happy to fully explain to the children's authorities why I believe my son's current living conditions are unacceptable.'

Gio was threatening her. Gio was actually telling her that he was prepared to report her to the social services for what he evidently saw as inadequate or neglectful childcare. The very thought made Billie shake with rage, a flush running across her cheekbones, her chin up, her green eyes defiant. 'Well, maybe you'd be happy to tell me because quite frankly I don't know what your problem is!'

'You are living with a prostitute and leaving my child in her care. I will not tolerate that,' he asserted with icy precision.

Off-balanced by that condemnation coming at her out of nowhere, Billie sank weakly down on the sofa, her legs suddenly giving way beneath her. It had not occurred to her that a routine investigation of her life would also dig up Dee's biggest secret. Pale, her clear eyes reflecting her strain and distress, she stared back at Gio. 'Dee's a bartender now. She's put her past behind her...'

'I don't put a time limit on a past like that, nor do I want such a woman in close contact with my son or taking care of him,' Gio delivered with inflexible cool.

'People make mistakes, people change, turn their lives around. Don't be so narrow-minded!' Billie urged, stricken, appalled that he had uncovered her cousin's troubled history and leapt straight to a disparaging conclusion.

Dee had got involved with an older man in her teens and had dropped out of school and ended up as a drug addict on the streets. Dee had been brutally honest with Billie about her past and Billie had tremendous respect for the amount of work and effort the other woman had put into making a fresh start for her and the twins.

'I'm glad for her sake that she's turned her life around but I still don't want her anywhere near my son,' Gio growled without apology. 'How do you know she's not still turning tricks at the bar where she works at night?'

'Because I know her and how much she values what she has now!' Billie slammed back furiously.

'I want my son out of this house right now,' Gio admitted. 'I want the two of you to move into my hotel with me until we get this situation sorted out.'

Wildly disconcerted by that demand, Billie stared back at him. 'No,' she said straight away.

'Say no and take the consequences,' Gio drawled softly, chillingly.

'What's that supposed to mean?'

'That I will use whatever I have against you to make the case for gaining custody of my son,' Gio advanced with measured force. 'I will go to social services with my concerns and they are bound by law to investigate.'

'I don't believe I'm hearing this!' Billie exclaimed jerkily, appalled by what he was telling her and cringing at the prospect of Dee being investigated once again by suspicious hypercritical officials, who would disinter the past that Dee had worked so hard to leave behind her. 'You're threatening me and my cousin!'

'If it is in my son's best interests, there's nothing I won't do for his benefit,' Gio intoned harshly. 'He is my primary concern here. I don't care what it takes or who else it hurts but I will always do my absolute best for him by whatever means possible.'

'How can you feel like that about a son you haven't even met yet?' Billie demanded shakily.

'Because he has my blood in his veins. He is mine, he is a Letsos and I must fight his battles for him because it is my duty to do that while he is still too young to have a voice.' Gio glanced down at the wafer-thin gold watch barely visible below his immaculate white shirt cuff. 'You have fifteen minutes to pack.'

'Leaving here is absolutely out of the question.'

'No, it is your one chance to escape the penalty for defying me. If I leave this house without my son today, I will fight to win custody and I will use whatever means are at my disposal,' Gio warned her with chilling bite.

Her eyes rounding, Billie's upper lip parted company from her lower. 'You're not being reasonable!'

'Why would I be? You've stolen the first fifteen months of my son's life from me,' Gio pronounced with lethal cool. 'How can you be surprised that I refuse to allow you to steal one day more?'

In receipt of that caveat, Billie could feel the blood draining slowly from below her skin, shock smacking through her in a dizzy wave. He was angry, he was bitter, but he couldn't possibly be thinking through what he was doing. 'Are you crazy? Theo needs *both* of us,' she told him tightly.

His lean, strong face clenched hard. 'Of course he does…in a perfect world. And this, I need hardly remind you, is not a perfect world.'

'Where are you planning to make time for a baby in your schedule?' Billie demanded with scorn. 'You won't. You don't really want him. You're behaving as if Theo is some kind of a trophy.'

'*Pack,*' Gio urged, one long brown forefinger tapping his watch face. 'You need only bring what you need for twenty-four hours. Naturally I will cover any necessities you need.'

Frozen to the spot, Billie stared at him, unwilling to believe that he could threaten everything she held dear in her life on the strength of what could only be a whim. 'Gio—'

'Not one word,' Gio cut in fiercely. 'I *want* my son. You've had all the time with him that you ever wanted. It's my turn now and I'm taking it.'

Billie reached a sudden decision. She would go to the hotel and allow Gio the time and space to get acquainted with Theo. Surely that major concession would cool his temper and calm him down? Sadly, she couldn't feel sure of the outcome. Gio's anger was shockingly new to her and she could still feel that anger sizzling from him in invisible sparks that could ignite into an explosion. Right now, opposition would probably only make him angrier and given a few hours' respite he would surely cool off and develop a more practical outlook, she reasoned frantically.

Billie withdrew a case from the hall cupboard and carried it up to her room. She packed the basics for herself and her son and then went downstairs to throw Theo's feeding essentials into a holdall. In the kitchen she scribbled a note to Dee, telling her where she had gone and that she would phone.

'Dee won't be able to work tonight if I'm not here to babysit for her,' Billie protested as she pulled on a light cotton jacket. Beneath the onslaught of Gio's appraisal she suddenly felt like a complete mess and she turned her head away, stiff with self-loathing. Her toffee-coloured corkscrew curls were never going to compare to Calisto's blade-straight blonde locks. Her hips were never going to be boyishly lean, nor would her boobs ever be dainty handfuls. Short of a body transplant, she was what she was. Wearing only a smattering of make-up, she looked very ordinary. It was ironic that she was so casually dressed because she hadn't wanted Gio to think that she had made a special effort for him. It was not a comfort that looking less than her best now felt like striking an own goal.

'I'll hire a babysitter for your cousin.'

'I can't let her down like this, Gio. It took so long for her to find a job with hours that suited.'

'I said I'll take care of it and I will,' Gio incised, grabbing her case from the hall and yanking open the front door, determined to let nothing come between him and his ultimate objective. 'Trust me.'

His chauffeur was waiting on the step to collect her case. After a moment's hesitation, Billie passed over her holdall as well, snatched a tiny jacket off the handles of the pram below the stairs and went up to lift Theo out of his cot. *Trust me!* Perhaps the strangest thing was that she *did* trust Gio because he had told her the truth even when she didn't want to hear it and he had never broken his word to her.

Her son was sleepy and warm as toast. She nuzzled her cheek against his smooth skin and breathed in his glorious baby scent before threading his short little arms into the jacket. Even in the very dark mood he was in, Gio had stated that their son needed both of his parents, she reminded herself staunchly. He wasn't trying to split them up; he was only making threats to make her listen and do what he wanted. Possibly all he really wanted was a couple of days with free access to Theo so that he could get to know him and he couldn't have that opportunity without including Billie in the arrangements.

A built-in safety seat for a child sat in the rear seat of the limousine. Billie settled Theo in and did up the buckle while her son craned his head to stare at Gio with big brown eyes. Silence fell while the two of them sized each other up. Gio had a cell phone in his hand and the light danced across the metallic finish. Theo stretched out a hand to grab the phone and Billie was incredulous when Gio handed it over.

'You can't give him that!' Billie exclaimed as the phone went straight into Theo's mouth to be chewed. 'He tries to eat everything.'

Billie filched the phone back. Theo looked at his empty hand and wailed while Billie passed the phone back to Gio out of her son's view. She dug a toy out of the holdall to give her son. He studied it with a jutting lower lip and threw it down.

'He wants the phone back,' Gio breathed in wonderment.

'Of course he does…it's got lots of buttons. The brightest, shiniest new toy always gets his interest.'

They drew up outside the hotel. Billie climbed out

and leant back into the car to unbuckle Theo but Gio was one step ahead of her and was already hoisting Theo into his arms. She followed them into the hotel. Theo loved new places just as much as new toys and his curly dark head was turning this way and that with keen interest. Billie stepped into the lift. Theo beamed at her from the vantage point of his father's arms, clearly very pleased with the exchange.

Billie was surprised to enter a different suite from the one that Gio had previously used. 'Have you changed to another floor?'

'Of course, we needed more space,' Gio pointed out while Theo frantically wriggled in his arms. With a sigh, Gio gave way and gently lowered Theo to the wooden floor. The little boy crawled off at high speed, grabbed at the leg of a fancy sofa and hauled himself upright, grinning with satisfaction.

'Theo's a clever boy,' Billie praised warmly.

Her son's sturdy little legs began to wobble and he toppled down onto his bottom in a sudden loss of balance and burst into floods of tears. Gio scooped him up again and held him high above his head. In his usual mercurial fashion, Theo forgot his moment of misery and burst out laughing instead at finding himself airborne. Gio made aeroplane noises like a little boy and whirled his son energetically round the room while Billie watched with a dropped jaw, not entirely sure that she could credit what she was seeing. Gio, shedding his dignity and distance, Gio smiling with unabashed enjoyment.

'It's time he had lunch,' Billie remarked.

The game between father and son concluded. A high chair was delivered along with the case and Billie started to feed Theo, who wanted to feed himself and complained vociferously between mouthfuls until she finally gave him the spoon. Theo stuck the spoon in the carton of yogurt with a victorious smile. Billie was still in a daze, her mind still engaged in replaying Gio acting as she had never before seen him act. Only an hour earlier, he had been threatening her with an adverse report to social services.

It had been an utterly ruthless threat that had chilled Billie to the marrow. A couple of years earlier, before Dee began getting her life straightened out, Dee's children had been put into care. Although she had got the twins back again and no longer even received visits to check on her progress, any allegation of negligent childcare made against the household where Dee lived would certainly result in a full investigation being made by the authorities. Billie could not bear the threat of that happening to her cousin again. It would flatten Dee's confidence, make her feel like an unfit mother again and if people realised that social services were checking up on her it would rouse local gossip. There was very little that Billie would not have done to protect Dee from such a development.

Yet the same male who had voiced that chilling threat had shown an entirely different side of himself to their son. With Theo, Gio had been playful, uninhibited, almost joyful, three traits she would never ever have associated with Gio's cool, calm and reserved nature. She recognised that Gio's interest in his son was considerably more powerful than she had ever dreamt it would be and she wondered uneasily where that left her in the triangle. He had said he wanted his son. What exactly did that mean?

Gio strode into one of the rooms leading off the spacious reception room and reappeared in jeans and a trendy striped cotton sweater. Billie couldn't drag her eyes from his lean, dark, devastating face as he watched entranced while Theo piled up his bricks and smashed them down again, giggling at the noise he was making. The tight jeans delineated every muscle in Gio's long, powerful thighs and narrow hips as he squatted down on the floor beside Theo. Billie's gaze ran over his washboard-flat stomach to the bulge below his belt and she averted her eyes, as hot and cold as someone with a fever. And mortifyingly, she knew precisely what was wrong with her. The kind of craving she had for Gio didn't go away, didn't take a back seat when you wanted it to, didn't fade when you knew it should; it just went on and on, the gift that kept on giving.

Sometimes wanting Gio had felt like a life sentence to Billie. Her pregnancy had only accelerated her exit from his life because she had been afraid that he might guess her secret. She had believed that that would be the ultimate humiliation because she had assumed that Gio would foist all the blame on her for her inconvenient pregnancy and make her feel dreadful as well as guilty and unworthy. Yet now he was telling her differently, insisting that he would never have suggested she have a termination.

Yet how much faith could she have in what Gio was currently saying? Gio, after all, was speaking with the benefit of hindsight, aware that his dynastic marriage was destined to fail. But two years ago that marriage had been very important to him and Billie's pregnancy would have been a severe embarrassment at the very least. What on earth had he meant when he had sworn he would never have married had he known about Billie's pregnancy?

It would never have occurred to Billie then that she could set the clock forward by two years and would see Gio, down on his jeans-clad knees, creating a precarious tower of bricks for Theo's benefit and actually laughing when Theo smacked it down with a chubby fist.

'You said you wanted Theo,' Billie murmured quietly, having finally worked up the courage to press for answers. 'What does that mean exactly?'

'That now that I've found him, I'm not walking away again,' Gio intoned, level dark golden eyes resting on her above Theo's head. Such beautiful eyes he had that even thinking was a challenge when she looked at them.

'No...er obviously,' she managed gruffly, 'you want to get to know him and stay in contact.'

Keeping very still, Gio lifted an ebony brow. 'I want much more than that.'

'How much more?' she pressed, struggling to breathe while level with those stunning eyes of his.

A sardonic smile curled Gio's wide sensual mouth. 'I don't like half measures…I want it *all*.'

'And what does "all" encompass?' Billie asked shakily.

Gio surveyed her with grim amusement. He had thought she would work it out for herself. He was ready to give her what she had always wanted from him and what he had never dreamt of offering before. Now he had very sound reasons for offering and anything else he gained as a by-product did not have to be measured or considered. The ever-ready pulse at his groin grew heavy while his attention roved to the deep valley between her full breasts, which was tantalisingly visible every time she angled her head down to speak to him. He wanted to rip her clothes off and slide between her thighs and stay there until he had worked off the powerful hunger riding him.

'Gio…?' she prompted, crystalline green eyes very serious.

'I want it all…as in marriage,' Gio filled in smoothly, long fingers smoothing back the curls on Theo's brow as his son slumped back against him for support. 'It's the only serviceable option we have.'

CHAPTER SIX

'LET ME GET this straight...' Billie framed between bloodless lips, barely able to credit what he was implying. 'You're suggesting that *we* get *married*?'

'If we marry, Theo's birth is automatically legitimised under British law.'

'But that scarcely matters when anyone who knows his age will guess that he was born while you were married to another woman,' Billie pointed out flatly.

'That's immaterial. The end result is what I want most—Theo legitimised, his place as my heir legally secured and recognised,' Gio spelt out very quietly, his dark, velvet drawl lowered to the level of an insidious husky murmur. 'That is his birthright and I want him to have it.'

'Even if it means you have to marry me to achieve that?' Billie prompted in disbelief.

'You will marry me for his sake and I will marry you for the same reason. We're responsible for his birth and we should put him first,' Gio told her squarely. 'We owe him that.'

Her skin clammy with disconcertion, Billie was

trembling where she sat. Long, long ago, she had dreamt of being Gio's wife, indeed she had dreamt the whole fairy tale before being forced to accept in the most painful way possible that it was just a fantasy. She could hardly bring herself to accept that he was actually talking about marrying her because it was like opening a locked door to let the silly fairy tale back in. She wrapped her arms protectively round herself. 'And you're quite sure that Theo's rights as your heir couldn't be secured any other way?'

'I could have legal agreements drawn up to officially acknowledge him as my son but nothing of that nature would be as watertight as marriage to his mother. In such agreements there is almost always a loophole or an irregularity and a clever enough lawyer can always find those weaknesses and build on them to make a claim.'

'And who on earth do you think is likely to make a claim?' Billie pressed in wonderment, sufficiently challenged to even picture her infant son as a child of future means.

'Have you any idea how wealthy I am?' Gio asked with lethal quietness of tone. 'Or of the lengths even wealthy people will go to in an effort to enrich themselves or their children even more?'

'Probably not,' she conceded ruefully, knowing when she was out of her depth.

'When I was fourteen, my stepmother tried to have me disinherited from the family trust in favour of her son, who was eight years old. The claim was only thrown out of court when my grandfather was able to prove that *her* son was not his grandson,' Gio completed.

Billie was sharply disconcerted, never having had any suspicion that Gio's place in his family had been challenged before he even reached adulthood. She frowned, shaken on Gio's behalf, wondering what on earth his childhood could have been like with such a spiteful and grasping stepmother and finally comprehending his fears on Theo's behalf.

'We can get married within a matter of days,' Gio told her smoothly, as if he had already worked out that he had won the battle. 'After the ceremony, we'll fly out to Greece and I'll introduce my wife and child to my family.'

Quite unable to credit such an event even taking place with her in a starring role, Billie sprang out of her seat and walked over to the window. 'That would be crazy, me trying to pretend I was your wife… We can't do this!'

'You will *be* my wife, you won't be pretending. What it comes down to is…how much do you love your son?' Gio enquired with almost casual cruelty.

Billie went rigid. 'That's not fair!'

'Isn't it? You *chose* to make yourself solely responsible for Theo and his future happiness. I'm only asking you to make good on your mistakes and ensure that he receives everything that should be his by right of birth,' he asserted glibly.

Billie inwardly squirmed at the accusation that she had made a serious mistake where Theo was concerned in not immediately informing Gio that he had a child, but the reference to Greece had sent her thoughts racing in another direction. 'If the marriage is only a legal formality why would you need me to accompany you to Greece?'

'Would you allow me to take Theo to Greece without you?' Gio asked in apparent surprise.

'*No!*' Billie proclaimed instantly.

'And while the marriage may appear to be little more than a legal formality to you,' Gio continued in the same reasonable tone, 'it is essential that it appears to be a normal marriage.'

Billie closed her arms round herself again, feeling threatened, cornered, bewildered, fighting that disorientation on every level as her chin tilted and her green eyes flared bold and bright as emeralds. 'But why should it have to appear normal?' she demanded.

'Do you want our son to feel guilty when he's older that you were forced to marry me for his benefit?' Gio enquired.

Billie frowned. 'Of course not—'

'Making it seem normal is a whitewash. There's nothing I can do about that,' Gio swore, manipulating the argument to the very best of his ability, flexing a level of cunning he had never utilised on Billie before. 'The more people who accept that the marriage is normal, the fewer the awkward questions that will be asked and the less comment it will create.'

'Nobody's going to accept that you freely *chose* to marry your mistress!' Billie slashed back at him angrily, hating to use that label on herself but willing to use it if it forced him to see sense.

'But we are the only people who know that you were my mistress. We didn't broadcast the fact and now we can be grateful that we kept a low profile. *Ne*...yes, you've had my child,' Gio conceded, sliding fluidly upright and moving towards her. 'All that proves is that we had a relationship.'

Billie clashed with spectacular dark eyes and her heart raced. 'All that proves is that we had, at least, a one-night stand.'

'*Diavelos*...you're not a one-night-stand woman and no man looking at you could believe that one night would be enough, *pouli mou,*' Gio purred soft and low, closing his hands firmly over hers to draw her close to his lean, powerful body. 'You will be my wife, the mother of my son. You will have nothing to be embarrassed about…'

It was a seductive image because Billie had always been embarrassed about the reality of her relationship with Gio. He had not been her knight on a white horse and she had not been his one true love. Her power had never stretched beyond the bedroom door and that was a demeaning truth that Billie had always felt shamed by, for what sort of woman settled for that kind of half-relationship? Her hands trembled in the grasp of his. A whitewash, he called it. But to the woman whose heart he had broken, and in spite of the fact that love wasn't involved, it still seemed more like a fairy tale to be offered what he had once tacitly refused to offer her.

'I can't leave Dee or the shop to go to Greece,' Billie told him abruptly. 'It's impossible. The shop is my livelihood and I can't just up and leave it…'

Gio closed his arms round her. Freed, one of her hands skimmed up over his muscular torso and came to rest uncertainly on a broad shoulder while the other lifted of its own volition to delve into his cropped black hair. 'I'll look after everything,' he told her.

'I have to have my independence,' Billie muttered unsteadily, her mouth drying and her breathing quickening as he ran the tip of his tongue along the closed seam of her lips. Her mouth tingled, stinging tightness pinching her nipples to send a current of liquefied heat into her pelvis. 'Listen to me, Gio,' she urged even as her fingers massaged his well-shaped skull, fluffing up the short strands of hair that were never allowed to amount to curls.

Gio rocked his hips lightly against hers and she tensed, suddenly insanely aware of his arousal and her own. 'Theo's my son. It's my duty to look after *both* of you.'

With a mighty effort of self-control, Billie yanked herself back from Gio and temptation. He could always make her want him but she could not afford to be stretched thin by that fierce wanting while she was trying to concentrate on the need to conserve her own life. With a slight shudder of loss, she straightened her slight shoulders and breathed in deep and slow to compose her scattered wits.

'Sell the shop or let me hire a manager for it. You decide which option will suit you best,' Gio urged, his lean dark features taut with impatience.

Billie looked at him with wide eyes of disbelief.

'Gio…I worked very hard to build up my business. You can't expect me to walk away from it.'

'Not even for Theo?' Gio prompted, glancing down at the little boy now clinging precariously to his jeans-clad leg and gazing up at both of them. 'Our son needs both of us and will do for some time. I want a normal family rapport with him. At the very least you will have to relocate your life to London, so that I can have regular access to him.'

Unexpectedly that statement jolted Billie because Gio spent most of his time in Greece. No, he was definitely not offering her a fairy-tale for-ever marriage because he was clearly already envisaging a future in which they were separated and sharing custody of their son. Billie paled, feeling as though he had slapped her in the face with reality, but ironically it was her own silly thoughts she needed to put a guard on, she conceded painfully. Of course, Gio wasn't suggesting a real marriage and a whitewash marriage would naturally have a sell-by date beyond which it was no longer required.

'I need to think about all this,' Billie admitted tightly. 'You're talking about turning my life upside down.'

'And my own,' Gio added softly. 'None of this was on my bucket list either.'

That obvious fact struck Billie like a second slap when she least required it. She did not need the reminder that Gio would never have chosen to marry her were it not for Theo. That reality was engraved on her soul because he had once rejected her in favour of Calisto. She bent down and scooped up Theo, loving the warm cuddliness of his solid little body and using it as a comfort to the chill spreading through her stomach. 'I need to change him,' she explained, walking away to scoop up the holdall and locate the nearest bathroom.

Why were women so complicated? Gio thought in seething frustration. He had offered her what he had assumed she had always wanted and she was behaving as if he had offered her a dirty deal. What did she have to think about? How many women had to run off to the bathroom and change a nappy before they could decide whether or not they wanted to marry a billionaire? Was it possible that she suspected that he had a motivation that he wasn't sharing?

His lean, strong face set like granite. Admittedly, he had not told her the whole truth, could not possibly tell her the whole truth because that would make her fear him. He was fighting for what he believed in, fighting for what Theo needed most. In every battle there were winners and losers and Gio had no plans to be a loser or to stand by powerless while Theo received less than his due. In the rarefied world of the super-rich Billie could only be a trusting babe in arms. She was so ignorant of the utter ruthlessness that could make Theo a target for the greedy that she had no concept of how best to protect their son. But Gio knew and there was nothing he would not do to achieve that objective.

Billie hovered by the vanity while Theo crawled across the tiled floor and pulled himself up on the

side of the bath. Her brain was in turmoil, inescapable
fear rammed down behind every thought. Gio wanted
her to marry him for Theo's sake and she wanted to
give her son the best possible start in life. But there
would be a steep price to pay for such a rise in her social status, she acknowledged unhappily. She would
inevitably be an embarrassment to Gio, and his precious family were certain to disapprove of her. But
then doubtless Gio planned to pension her off once
all the legalities and his son's place in life had been
affirmed. So, it wouldn't be a real for-ever marriage
and would probably be set aside once Theo was old
enough to go and visit his father without his mother
in tow. Everything, she assumed, would happen exactly the way Gio wanted it to happen because he
left nothing to chance. She foresaw that reality and
froze at the terrifying prospect of being left so powerless, shorn of her home and her business. Did she
have a choice? Could she trust Gio with their son's
future well-being?

Theo anchored on her hip, Billie walked back into
the gracious reception room. Gio had removed his
jacket, loosened his tie and pushed up the sleeves of
his white silk shirt. The super-fine expensive ma-
terial accentuated the muscles that rippled with his
every movement and his impossibly taut, flat stomach. Her gaze lingered there, feverish memories of
torrid moments awakening, fingers and lips gliding
along his hard ribcage, smoothing over his abdomen
before stroking down the furrow of silky hair disappearing below his waistband. Her tummy flipped

and she gave herself a stern, frowning little shake as she emerged from her reverie. Black lashes flicking up on shrewd eyes, Gio completed the phone call he was making and set the phone down.

'OK. I'll marry you,' Billie spelled out tautly, her colour high. 'But that means I'm trusting you not to do anything that might harm Theo or me. If I find out that I can't trust you I'll leave you.'

Gio flashed her a deeply appreciative smile. She would never leave him again. Not unless she was prepared to leave her son behind with him, he reflected with immense satisfaction. She might not know it yet but her days of running were at an end.

'And you have to be totally, one hundred per cent faithful,' Billie decreed.

'I always was with you,' Gio responded airily.

'But there's that saying about how when a man marries his mistress he creates a vacancy,' Billie remarked flatly, her lush mouth compressing on a sense of humiliation.

'I think my life is complicated enough,' Gio fielded.

And of course he wouldn't be expecting to be married to her until he was old and grey and, since he would always have an end to their arrangement in sight, straying through boredom was less likely to be a problem, Billie affixed grimly, striving not to be hurt by that truth.

'Now that you've got what you wanted, can I go home?' Billie pressed.

'I want you here. Presumably you want to be in-

volved in making your own wedding arrangements.'
A straight ebony brow inclined. 'We'll have a small
wedding in the Greek Orthodox church I attend in
London. I've already applied for the required li-
cences.'

Billie's eyes flared in surprise. 'You took a lot for
granted.'

Gio's steady gaze held hers. 'I can afford to. Why
would you refuse to marry me when that was presumably what you wanted two years ago?'

Billie reddened as though she had been slapped.
So, he had finally worked that obvious fact out, had
he? Mortification drenched her like a tidal wave. 'I
don't buy into fairy tales any more.'

'But I want you to *have* the fairy tale, *pouli mou*,'
Gio breathed curtly, thoroughly disconcerting her
with that statement. 'I want you to wear a fancy dress
and all the trimmings.'

'Why? Because it will look good in the photos?'
Billie forced her strained eyes away from him, her
heart-shaped face stiff because she knew that he could
never give her the fairy tale. After all, the one essential facet of her fairy-tale denouement had been his
love. She was also wounded that he was so sure that
she would have married him like a shot two years
earlier, particularly when he had coolly turned away
from her to marry another, more suitable woman.
Her love had meant nothing to him in those days but
then she had offered her love too freely. Was it fair to
judge him harshly for not being able to love her back?

'A normal marriage,' he reminded her quietly. 'That is what I want and that is what we will have.'

His uncompromising arrogance set Billie's teeth on edge. Even though he was divorced he still had no fear of matrimonial failure. But then he wanted Theo and he wanted her, Billie conceded ruefully, and she knew that high-voltage libido of Gio's probably drove him harder than love ever could. He was, to say the least, an electrifyingly sexual personality. Had he ever loved Calisto? Or merely wanted the beautiful blonde? What had ultimately killed that wanting? And what did it matter to Billie? After all, she was only finally getting that wedding ring by default.

Gio's business team arrived to work with him that afternoon while Billie viewed images of wedding dresses online, sent at Gio's behest by a well-known designer. She squirmed over taking her measurements and sending them off and then buried the memory by picking her dream dress, her dream veil and her dream shoes while planning a timely trip to her favourite lingerie shop. But when she headed for the door with Theo in her arms, Gio asked coolly, 'Where are you going?'

'I have some shopping to do,' Billie told him, soft mouth settling into a firm line. 'And I want to do it with Dee.'

His stunning gaze iced over. 'No,' he said simply as he scrawled his signature on a document placed in front of him by an aide.

'Yes,' Billie said equally simply and walked on out of the door.

'Billie!' Gio roared down the corridor after her as she headed to the lift.

With reluctance she turned.

'I said no,' Gio reminded her icily.

Green eyes sparkling, Billie wandered back closer. 'And I wasn't going to argue with you in front of your staff but I have to see Dee.'

'You know I've arranged for a sitter for her for the next two weeks.'

'She's my cousin and my friend and she has always been there for me when I needed her,' Billie countered gently. 'I don't care what you say or how you feel about it but I will *not* turn my back on her.'

'Then leave Theo with me,' Gio urged, reaching out to take his son.

Billie retained a hold on Theo. 'You couldn't look after him on your own—'

'I won't be on my own. I hired a nanny. She's in the hotel right now awaiting my call.'

His interference, his conviction that he knew what was best for her child, made Billie bridle. 'Then you've wasted your time and your money because I will not leave Theo with a stranger.'

'I'll tell her to come up and you can meet her.'

Billie pursed her lips. 'Theo comes with me. Sorry, if you don't like that, but that's the way it's going to be.'

'Don't try to fight me,' Gio warned her softly. 'If

you fight, I will fight back and inevitably you'll get hurt.'

'Nothing you do could hurt me now,' Billie declared staunchly, refusing to be intimidated. 'And why don't you quit while you're ahead, Gio? I've agreed to turn my whole life upside down, to marry you and meet your family. How much more do you want or expect? When do *you* learn to compromise?'

'I don't,' Gio said succinctly, his strong jaw line squared. 'Not when it comes to my son and your involvement with an individual I don't want you mixing with.'

'That individual you don't want me mixing with was with me when I was in labour for two endless days!' Billie snapped back at him in a low intense voice that shook with emotion. 'She was there for me and Theo when you weren't and I was darned glad to have her!'

An almost imperceptible pallor spread beneath Gio's bronzed skin and his thick lashes screened his gaze to grim darkness. 'I would have been there for you if you'd told me you were pregnant—'

'I don't think so, Gio. You were a newly married man back then,' Billie reminded him without any expression at all.

'Go, then, if it means so much to you,' he urged with chilling bite.

'It *does* mean that much to me. I'm always loyal to my friends,' Billie declared with quiet dignity.

Gio glowered at her, lustrous dark eyes shimmering gold. 'Once, first and foremost, you were loyal to me.'

Billie dealt him a wry look. 'And where did that loyalty get me at the end of the day?' she quipped, stepping into the lift.

Gio wanted to snatch her back out of the lift and Theo with her but her reference to that word, 'compromise' had sunk in. He had ninety per cent of what he wanted and he would have the whole once they were married. In the short term, he could afford to be generous, he told himself sternly. But Billie had changed and he could no longer ignore the fact. She was ready to go toe-to-toe with him and fight. In some ineffable way she had grown up and the girl who had looked at him with starry eyes as if he were a knight in shining armour was no more. He didn't like that one little bit.

Even less did Gio appreciate the way he was feeling, shaken up and stirred, insanely abandoned by her departure, all reactions totally at war with the cool, adult, detached reserve with which he preferred to view the world. Above all, he didn't like people to get too close; he didn't want or miss the messy emotional responses that encouraged weakness, self-delusion and loss of control. He could only be content when calm and discipline ruled.

So, what was it about Billie that could make him feel so at odds with himself? She disturbed him, made him overreact, he decided grimly, hoping that that was a temporary affliction he would soon overcome. It seemed particularly ironic that she was also the only woman who had ever given him a sense of peace and contentment. But that was *not* the effect she was having on him at present. He had a great deal of work to accomplish before he could hope to take time off after the wedding. Mulling over the problem and the challenges, Gio was quick to decide that it would be more sensible to take a short break from Billie and the unwelcome and disturbing hothouse emotions she unleashed.

'You can't give me the house,' Dee told Billie squarely. 'I'm not going to live off you. I can afford to pay rent.'

Billie was reluctant to hurt her cousin's feelings by pointing out that once she was married to Gio she would have little use for the rental payment. Dee was fiercely independent and had learned young that she had to be that way. The few times she had depended on others, Dee had been let down.

'Are you hoping to sell the shop as a going concern?' Dee asked.

'It's as much my baby as Theo is,' Billie admitted. 'I really don't want to part with it at all.'

Dee looked at her anxiously and then, biting her lower lip, leant forward. 'Would you let me try to run it for a three-month trial period?' she asked hesitantly. 'I picked up quite a bit from you when I was helping you set it up and as long as I used a bookkeeper I think I could manage.'

Billie studied the blonde woman in surprise, never having suspected that her cousin had a yen to work in the shop. 'I had no idea you would be interested.'

'Well, I am interested, always have been to be honest…but I knew you couldn't afford a full-time employee, so there wasn't much point mentioning it.'

The two women talked at length and an agreement was reached. Billie was smiling by the end of their discussion, happy to think of Dee taking over her business, much preferring that to the option of selling.

'If you're willing to go to Greece, you must really trust Gio,' Dee remarked.

'He's always been straight with me, even when I didn't want to hear what he had to say,' Billie pointed out wryly. 'If he's prepared to marry me for Theo's benefit, I'm prepared to trust him.'

'You've got far too big a heart, Billie. Don't let him hurt you again,' Dee warned her worriedly.

It was a piece of advice that Billie wished she could take to heart after she returned to the hotel and discovered that Gio had checked out to fly back to London 'to work'. Not that she was fooled by the piece of fiction in the brief note he left for her. She had annoyed Gio and he had turned his back on her and walked away. She was familiar with the withdrawal of approval and presence that always followed such demonstrations of independent action. Once long ago she had insisted on attending a tutorial interview while he was staying at the apartment. He had been irritated that she should want to go out and leave him, even if it was only for a couple of hours. By the time she had got back, he had returned to Greece. Lesson learned, she had thought then, sick with disappointment and resolving never to mention the need to go anywhere else again. This time around, however, Billie was exasperated and furious that he had removed her from the comfort of home and familiarity and marooned her in a luxury hotel with a nanny and a four-strong set of bodyguards to watch over her and Theo.

CHAPTER SEVEN

LEANDROS CONISTIS VERY nearly dropped his drink. 'You're getting married again?' he repeated like a well-trained parrot to the male who had so recently told him he would never remarry.

Gio dealt his best friend a forbidding look that dared irreverent comment. '*Ne*...yes.'

'Do I know the lady?' Leandros enquired somewhat stiffly.

'You met her briefly on one occasion,' Gio divulged grudgingly. 'Her name's Billie...'

Leandros knocked what remained of his drink down in one suicidal gulp because he knew in that same moment that Canaletto's name would never ever cross his lips again. 'I didn't realise...Billie was still a feature in your life. Have your family met her?' he asked.

Gio compressed his wide sensual mouth. 'No.'

'And when is this wedding at which you wish me to act as your best man to take place?'

'Tomorrow.' Gio threw in the necessary details of place and time in a demonstration of spectacular cool.

Leandros studied the date on his watch face, astonished that it wasn't the first of April and an April fool's joke because Gio, who was as a rule extremely conservative and never imprudent, had literally stunned him speechless. 'It seems…er…very sudden,' he commented cautiously.

'*Ne*…yes,' Gio conceded.

'Very…er hasty.' Leandros was gradually becoming more daring.

'Not hasty enough,' Gio told him drily. 'My son is fifteen months old.'

'Oh, Billie, you look amazing.' Dee sighed as she stepped back from tying the laces at the back of Billie's wedding gown.

Billie stared at her reflection in the cheval mirror and blinked several times at the still-unfamiliar furnishings of the opulent bedroom. Gio had taken a plush city apartment for her and Theo to stay in. She still couldn't quite believe that she was marrying Gio, indeed she kept on expecting some movie cameraman to show up and shout, 'Cut!' before things went any further. After all, in an hour's time she was going to marry a man she wasn't even speaking to. How's that for stupidity? she asked herself ruefully.

Gio had left her and Theo in the hotel in Yorkshire for four days. Of course he had made regular phone calls and had talked during those calls as though there were nothing wrong with his desertion while smoothly excusing himself in advance.

'I knew you had too much on your plate to accompany me down to London,' Gio had told her, ignoring the fact that he had put one of his aides in charge of dealing with all the wedding and removal arrangements for her.

'I knew you would want to spend time saying goodbye to your friends and sorting out your shop,' Gio had said optimistically, ignorant of the reality that Dee was walking Billie down the aisle while her twins were acting as a bridesmaid and pageboy.

'I knew that you would think it was a bad idea to subject Theo to another change of surroundings and more strangers when it wasn't strictly necessary,' Gio had opined complacently.

Billie was furious with him and her anger hadn't faded; it had only grown while Gio had acted as if leaving his bride-to-be and newly discovered son behind him in Yorkshire had been the only possible thing to do. Striving to keep a lid on that tight little knot of rage locked deep inside her, Billie surveyed her dress with faraway eyes. It was a romantic dress fashioned of Chantilly lace and chiffon, light and floaty and styled to make the most of her natural curves and waist. The flirty short veil and crown of flowers had a natural elegant simplicity. Pearl-studded shoes peeped out below the hem of her gown.

Someone knocked on the bedroom door. Since the only other person in the apartment was Irene, the pleasant middle-aged nanny whom Gio had hired, Dee answered it.

'Oh…' Dee backed off uneasily, her surprise unhidden when she recognised Gio.

Billie froze. 'You're not supposed to see me in my wedding dress!' she exclaimed in consternation.

Taken aback by Dee's appearance, Gio muttered a stiff acknowledgment in English while hungrily taking in the vision Billie made in her white dress. He had died and gone to heaven, he decided without hesitation. As Dee ducked out behind him, tactfully closing the door in her wake, he strode forward, his attention locked to the tantalising pout of Billie's ripe pink mouth and the creamy swell of her luscious breasts above the boned bodice of her gown. 'You look fantastic,' he breathed in a roughened undertone.

It was a challenge for Billie not to echo that sentiment. It might be a small wedding on Gio's terms, which was to say that it was a large wedding on *her* terms, but Gio had still chosen to embrace the formality of a full morning suit teamed with a striped black and silver cravat at his brown throat. The black jacket was exquisitely tailored to his tall, well-built form, delineating his broad shoulders and muscular chest, while the striped trousers enhanced his narrow hips and long powerful legs. Billie collided headily with smouldering dark golden eyes heavily fringed with curling black lashes. Gio looked absolutely gorgeous.

'What are you doing here?' she whispered and then tensed. 'Have you changed your mind? If you have, it's all right. I'm not going to make a fuss. It doesn't feel real anyway—'

'*Theos*…of course I haven't changed my mind!' Gio ground out, extending the jewel case he carried in one lean brown hand. 'I wanted to give you this…'

For a split second he too wondered what he was doing there for in truth he had acted on the kind of impulse he usually suppressed. On the way to the church he had realised that he *had* to see her before the wedding and there was nothing wrong with that, he reasoned uneasily, when he was about to take the very major step of marrying her. Desire was always an acceptable motivation as long as it stayed within rational bounds. And sex with Billie was incredible. He felt nothing else, needed nothing beyond her physical presence.

In a daze, Billie blinked and accepted the case, flipping it open to display a breathtaking triple string of pearls and dangling pearl earrings. The set would match her shoes and be a great deal more impressive than the cheap diamanté set she had purchased. 'It's beautiful,' she murmured weakly as he moved forward to detach the pearls from the case and fasten them round her neck.

His fingertips brushed the nape of her neck. 'I wanted to give you something special.'

The glowing pearls were cool at her throat and she bent over the case to detach the earrings. Threading her veil and her curls out of the way, she put the earrings on. 'Thank you,' she said woodenly, thinking that he hadn't changed one little bit in all the years she had known him. Here he was still trying to bribe and guilt her into ignoring his bad behaviour.

'I can't stand you talking to me in that chilly voice,' Gio informed her grimly. 'Obviously you're annoyed I left you behind in Yorkshire.'

Billie's teeth rattled together with rage. 'You mean…you actually noticed I was being cool on the phone?'

'Considering that you would once chat about nothing in particular for hours on end without the slightest encouragement, one-word responses *were* rather obvious,' Gio countered with sardonic emphasis. 'What's wrong with you? You never used to play games like that with me.'

'Shut up before I lose my temper!' Billie urged between clenched teeth, her facial muscles locked tight. 'You left me in that hotel with Theo and a bunch of bodyguards and a strange nanny!' she accused. 'You did it deliberately because I had annoyed you. You just took off for London. What happened to your all-consuming interest in getting to know your son? You *can't* just saunter in here and throw a bunch of priceless pearls at me and expect that to take the place of an apology and an explanation!' Billie launched at him in fiery denunciation.

'I have nothing to apologise for. Now that I have got on top of work, I will have far more time to spend with Theo and you *after* the wedding,' Gio told her stubbornly, watching her curls bounce round her animated features, the passion flaring in her green eyes, while noting how luminous the pearls were set against her creamy skin and the firm, sweet swell of her breasts. Hunger stormed through his tautening length in an uncontrollable wave, leaving him painfully aroused. 'I refuse to go through a wedding with you behaving like this. This is why I needed to see you.'

Billie was silenced. Suddenly she was the one at fault for straining their relationship beyond tolerance. Wide-eyed she stared back at him, the atmosphere dense and sending a curious little quiver through her belly. 'So…we…er call it off now and go our separate ways?' she whispered shakily.

Gio stared at her in rampant disbelief, his dark eyes golden-bronze spearheads of intimidation at the mere thought of her pulling a disappearing act again. 'You're not going anywhere without me.'

Billie didn't understand because that sudden shock of fear had destroyed her ability to think straight. Her heart was jumping up and down inside her ribcage like a rubber ball being bounced and making it very hard for her to breathe.

'*Ever again,*' Gio growled in menacing completion as he scooped her up in his arms and brought her down on the bed.

'What are you doing?' Billie gasped. 'Gio…*my dress*!'

Gio came down on top of her, almost squashing her flat. 'Stop struggling…you're more likely to rip something.'

Billie looked up at him with huge disconcerted eyes. 'Gio…we *can't*…this isn't the answer to anything.'

Gio rubbed his mouth sexily across hers with a sensual groan. 'It's the *only* answer for me.'

'You're wrecking my make-up,' she framed unevenly, fingertips dancing shyly through his cropped black hair, slowly dropping to frame his amazing cheekbones.

'You don't need make-up,' Gio told her thickly.

'Every bride needs make-up,' Billie argued, trying to slide unobtrusively out from beneath his weight without shredding her dress.

He lowered his head and devoured her mouth with a hungry driving urgency that made her every sense shift into superdrive with piercingly sweet longing. The taste and scent of him infiltrated her like a dangerous drug, blowing her control out of the water. 'I won't wreck the dress,' he promised, lifting his hips to tip the bundled skirt of her gown up to her waist.

'*Gio...*' Billie whispered pleadingly even as her back arched and her pelvis rocked up to his without her volition.

'*Diavelos*, Billie...I *hurt*,' he ground out, his breath fanning her cheek while he shifted revealingly against her, grinding the thrust of his erection into the cradle of her thighs.

And low down in her pelvis, deep in her feminine core a surge of moisture dampened her most tender flesh and she started to melt. 'We can't...we haven't got the time.'

'We'll make time,' he husked, yanking out his phone as it buzzed, clamping it to her ear and talking in fast Greek to a male voice that sounded both loud and agitated. 'Our day, nobody else's,' he spelled out fiercely.

Long fingers glided up her inner thigh, leaving

tingles of humming energy in their wake. Her eyes closing, her head fell back on the pillows, her neck extending as her spine arched. Her heart was racing thump-thump-thump at the foot of her throat. He stroked the taut triangle of satin between her thighs and the only thing in the world for her at that moment was the stupendous high of excitement and anticipation holding her fast. With a yank, Gio dislodged her bodice sufficiently to expose a creamy breast topped by a pale pink nipple. He closed his mouth urgently to that swollen peak and a stifled gasp escaped her, eyes squeezing tight shut.

'I need to know you're mine,' Gio growled against her throat.

He eased a finger below her lace-edged knickers and stroked along the petal-soft folds. Her thighs opened wider in helpless invitation and when he rubbed the little bud where she was most sensitive she moaned and shifted her hips, urging him on, helpless in the grip of the savage need he could induce. He thrust a long finger into her tight, wet sheath and she jerked, on the edge of crying out until he clamped his mouth to hers to silence the sounds she was making. The rhythmic play of his fingers over her tender flesh sent ripples of throbbing excitement through her. As the tension in her pelvis rose to an all-consuming ache that was unbearable, her every muscle clenched tight and she soared to a breathless shattering peak of ecstasy while biting the shoulder of his jacket to mute the sob of release building up inside her.

'Oh…' she mumbled afterwards, her body as languorous as a floating beach ball.

Gio's phone was screeching in his pocket. Scanning her dreamy face, he switched it off with an unsteady hand. Strangely, although he was still taut with sexual arousal, the inner tension driving him had dissolved. He felt like himself again for the first time in four days and snapped straight into rescue mode, propelling Billie off the bed, repositioning her bodice, brushing down the skirt of her gown before urging her into the bathroom where he stared in all male helplessness at the crushed veil hanging askew, the curls positively rioting round it and the smudges of the lipstick he had dislodged.

'Good grief,' Billie groaned, catching her mangled reflection. 'Gio, you're a menace.'

Gio washed with enviable cool and ran a comb through his tousled hair. A sharp knock sounded on the bedroom door and it opened the merest crack. 'The cars have arrived, Mr Letsos. We cannot be late…' It was Damon Kitzakis' voice.

'I'll get your friend to help you,' Gio breathed in sudden decision.

Billie was in full bridal panic mode, scanning her swollen mouth and tumbled hair and veil with withering scorn. You should have said no, she told herself furiously. Why didn't you say no? Why had she, once again, failed to call a halt? Sex had always been a slippery slope with Gio. She couldn't keep her hands off him, she couldn't resist his passion but she was convinced that he would respect her more if she was less spontaneous and more restrained. Yet he had received no satisfaction whatsoever from what they had done, she acknowledged in surprise as she waged a frantic war on her rebellious curls and hurriedly repaired her make-up.

Gio reappeared in the bathroom doorway, lean, strong face taut. 'Damon thought it best that your cousin, her children and Irene and Theo leave immediately for the church. You're travelling with Leandros and me.'

Billie turned from the mirror. 'But you and your best man are supposed to arrive *first*.'

'You can wait in the church porch for ten minutes, *koukla mou*,' Gio pointed out, lustrous dark eyes gleaming with sudden amusement. 'Why do you take all these silly little rules so seriously?'

Billie went pink and lifted her chin. 'I assume all brides do the same.'

Gio closed a hand over hers and pulled her towards the lift, sweeping her off her feet before she could reach the pavement and depositing her in a vast tumbling heap of lace and chiffon into the stretch limousine waiting by the kerb.

Billie forced a smile when Leandros Conistis looked at them both in frank astonishment. The heat of almost unbearable embarrassment engulfed her in a burning tide because she had never forgotten her one and only meeting with Gio's best friend and the incredulous look on his face that evening when he had realised that she had never heard of Canaletto.

Leandros tossed a handkerchief at Gio. 'You have lipstick on your face.'

Billie's mortification did not abate at that aside; indeed it worsened. Now the other man would think that she was not only stupid but also a slut with no idea of how to behave like a dignified bride. Even though she knew she was being ridiculously oversensitive, she could not overcome her attack of self-consciousness. Dee helped her climb out of the limousine and ushered her into the porch where she admired the pearl set, teased her cousin about what she saw as Gio's wildly romantic gesture at showing up at the apartment before the wedding and then fussed with the skirts of Billie's gown before checking that her daughter, Jade, was still carrying her basket and flowers and Davis, his lucky horseshoe.

Walking down the aisle of the half-empty church some minutes later, her hand resting lightly on her cousin's arm, Billie was earnestly instructing herself that she was not living a fairy tale and striving not to react to the lean dark charisma of Gio's sheer beauty as he looked down the aisle, brilliant dark eyes glimmering gold.

'This is your dream,' Dee whispered unhelpfully at that exact same moment. 'Stop fretting…enjoy your moment in the sun.'

Billie recalled the vanishing act that Gio had pulled in Yorkshire, her own frustrated rage, and breathed in deep. So, he wasn't straightforward, he was complex, secretive and arrogant, but as she focused on his tall, dark, powerful figure at the altar her heart sang its own deeply revealing signature tune. That was when she recognised and accepted the truth—the truth that vanity had made her deny. Gio was the man she loved, very probably would always be the man she loved, regardless of what he did in the future, because she was very steady in her affections.

Acknowledging the strength of her feelings was like breaking free of a constricting band round her chest. She had never got over Gio and now he was back and they had a child and she was about to become his wife. Instead of expecting, indeed almost inviting the roof to fall in on her, wasn't it time she went for a little positive thinking? And it was at that instant of sunny, optimistic thought with her emotions on a high that her eyes zeroed in on the blue-eyed blonde keenly studying her two pews back from the front. Her heart and her body froze in concert and even her feet became reluctant to do her bidding. Dee had to use momentum to move Billie on down the aisle.

Calisto was a guest at their very small wedding. Billie was in shock. What did Calisto's presence today of all days mean? Her hand trembled as Gio slid the ring onto her wedding finger. Her skin was clammy with shock, her knees in a rigid hold. In her mind's eye she was seeing not the priest but Calisto, her tiny proportions sheathed in a killer-blue fitted dress and lace jacket, a jaunty little feather confection adorning her head, waterfall-straight platinum-pale hair falling to her shoulders, framing a face of such perfection that angels would weep to look at it. In print she had been a beauty; in the flesh she was downright dazzling, setting a standard that Billie could never hope to reach. A deep chill spread through Billie like an unexpected frost on a summer day.

'What's your ex-wife doing here?' Billie whispered shakily on the church steps as the society photographer and his assistant got them to pose with linked hands.

Gio massaged the tender skin of her wrist with his thumbs, sending a delicious little thrill of awareness trickling through her tense body. 'Haven't a clue, but it wouldn't have been polite to ask her to leave.'

'Perhaps not.' Billie was in two minds about what being polite entailed in such circumstances. 'But how did she know about the wedding?'

Gio sent her a frowning glance. 'Naturally I told her about it. It would've been bad manners to let her find out from anyone else. Cal probably thinks that showing up is the socially "hip" thing to do. She likes to be "hip",' he completed drily.

Billie was sharply disconcerted by the news that Gio was still on good enough terms with his former wife to have automatically informed her of his remarriage. The comfortable way he referred to Calisto with the fond diminutive 'Cal' bothered her even more although she was quick to question her own reaction. Not all ex-wives and husbands loathed each other and it was perfectly possible that Calisto had turned up simply out of curiosity. And who could blame her for that? Gio and Calisto had only been divorced for a couple of months at most. She glanced across to where Calisto stood in animated conversation with Leandros and two other Greek friends.

'She's very friendly with everyone,' Billie remarked gingerly, quite frankly envying the blonde's confident assumption of her welcome. Calisto evidently didn't feel the slightest bit uncomfortable attending her ex-husband's wedding and Billie struggled to be equally accepting of the blonde's presence.

'Cal is Leandros' first cousin,' Gio advanced. 'And one of my lawyers is her stepbrother. She probably knows virtually everybody here.'

Dismay at those previously unknown close connections assailed Billie and her unease only increased when she saw Calisto climb with a tinkling girlish giggle into a limo with the three men. A wedding breakfast was being served at an exclusive London hotel. She seriously hoped Calisto wasn't going to push her way in there as well. It was a hope destined to disappointment, however, because the first person Billie saw in the foyer was Calisto, beaming smile all over her perfect face as she surged forward to kiss Gio on both cheeks and beg sweetly for an introduction to Billie.

'I've already met your son…what a little darling!' Calisto gushed, all dimples and flapping fake lashes. 'And what a clever, clever girl you are to have brought such a little angel into the world.'

Gio laughed softly. 'Theo's cute, isn't he?'

'*Super* cute,' Calisto purred in agreement, flexing manicured scarlet fingertips on Billie's arm to prevent her from moving away.

'Excuse us for a moment,' Dee interrupted in an undertone. 'Billie, you need your veil fixed. It's hanging by a thread.'

Relieved to have an excuse to escape, Billie followed her cousin to the other side of the foyer. She angled her head back to assist Dee's efforts to anchor her veil and she was in the perfect position to catch Dee's hissed enquiry, 'Who on earth is the pushy blonde?'

As Billie spun to fill in the details Dee's eyes got rounder and rounder. 'She's got a heck of a nerve coming today!' she commented angrily. 'No bride wants her predecessor as a guest!'

Billie coloured. 'I don't want to make a fuss about it when everybody else is quite happy.'

'By everybody else, you mean Gio,' Dee interpreted. 'She's spoiling your day and, like most men, he's just taking the easy way out by doing nothing!'

'He hates bitchiness and catfights. I'm not going to say anything,' Billie intoned as if she were mouthing a soothing mantra she badly needed to absorb. 'If Calisto can handle me then I can handle her.'

'Whatever you think,' Dee trilled, clearly unimpressed. 'But I wouldn't stand her being here like the spectre at the feast for longer than ten seconds.'

Billie greeted the other guests as they arrived with quiet poise. Several of Gio's British business colleagues were attending as well as his lawyers and a large group of London-based Greeks. She was surprised that he had not invited any of his family to attend their wedding and worried that they might have refused to attend because they disapproved of Gio marrying a woman from so ordinary a background.

She had met Gio's lawyers in Yorkshire when they had called at the hotel to present her with the pre-nuptial agreement. They had advised her to take independent advice before she signed but Billie really hadn't had the time to consult anyone, being far too busy packing up the life she had lived for two years and discarding what she no longer required. In any case, Gio was anything but mean when it came to money and, regardless of what might happen between them in the future, she didn't feel she needed documentary proof that he would always be fair. He had once mentioned that his father had been shamefully stingy in his monetary dealings with his mother after they had divorced and she was convinced he would never be guilty of committing the same sin.

As they ran out of guests to greet in the reception area beside the dining room, Billie saw Gio and Leandros approach Calisto. She watched that perfect face freeze and her scarlet-painted mouth open to deliver an obviously animated response before Billie forced herself to turn away and head for the cloakroom to freshen up. There was no denying that Calisto had cast a cloud over the day. Unfortunately, Calisto was Gio's ex and still part of his social circle and Billie was stuck with that reality. Making heavy weather of the fact wasn't going to change anything.

Billie was engaged in renewing her lipstick when the door slammed behind a new arrival and high heels smacked noisily across the tiles. Calisto ap-

peared in the mirror beside Billie like the evil fairy.
'Don't waste your time feeling smug that Gio's asked
me to leave. He's had long enough to regret our divorce and naturally he's upset at having to marry you
to get his son and even more upset to see you and
I together...well, there *is* no comparison, is there?'
Calisto pointed out, lifting her chin to examine her
perfect reflection with open admiration.

Billie turned away from the mirror, lifting her own
chin in fear that she might have a slight suggestion of
a double chin when she held her head at some angles
and that was a humiliation she could not have borne
in Calisto's presence. 'Gio divorced you?'

'Only because I wouldn't give him a baby,' Calisto told her cheerfully. 'But now that he's got one...
thank you *so* much for taking care of that problem for
me. He can have me *and* his precious son and heir.
You've given us a textbook solution to our dilemma.'

'What on earth are you trying to say?' Billie asked
in genuine astonishment.

'That triangles never work and it won't be long before Gio takes his son off you and reclaims me as his
wife,' Calisto trilled with satisfaction. 'You were his
mistress and I'm afraid the background of his life is
where a woman like you belongs.'

'A woman like me?' Billie prompted, her green
eyes taking on a dangerous sparkle.

'A tart with a heart,' Calisto quipped, rolling her
eyes. 'And let's not forget the pantomime big boobs
and bum. But you were never destined to be a Letsos
and your reign as one will be painfully short.'

Billie shook her head in silent wonderment as she walked to the door. How could Gio have married such a spiteful shrew? In comparison with Calisto, she was unquestionably rounder in certain areas but she was determined not to get drawn into a childish spat with the other woman. She was less sanguine, however, concerning Calisto's claims about Theo and why Gio had married her.

Was it possible that Gio had only married Billie to gain equal rights to his son? It was simply another angle to Gio's insistence that they marry to give Theo *his* birthright. Obviously Gio would benefit as well from the formal acknowledgement of his role as Theo's father. And was it true that Gio had divorced Calisto because she wouldn't give him a child? Stamping down on further conjecture about Calisto, Billie reminded herself comfortingly that Gio had asked his ex-wife to leave their wedding.

Feeling hot, flushed and distinctly out of sorts, Billie returned to the elegant function room and collected Theo from his nanny to give him a cuddle. While her son nestled close, she was relieved to see Gio and Leandros chatting away to Dee.

'She's pleasant,' Gio conceded later when they were all seated for the wedding breakfast. 'But that doesn't mean that I think she's a fit person for you to have as a friend.'

'Try to be less judgemental. If you hadn't seen that report, you wouldn't have known about her past,' Billie pointed out. 'And we've all made mistakes...you married Calypso.'

'Calisto,' Gio corrected. 'She's gone—'

'Good.' Lashes screening her gaze, Billie sipped her champagne.

'It wasn't appropriate for her to stay.'

'Why did you divorce her?' she heard herself ask.

'We were incompatible,' Gio fielded without hesitation.

'That's not telling me *any*—' Billie began heatedly as Gio lifted a hand and closed it into her curls to turn her back to him.

She clashed with smouldering dark golden eyes and a writhing inferno of heat rushed up inside her in response. Her heart stuttered, her breath shortened in her throat. The tip of his tongue traced the curve of her lower lip and the peaks of her full breasts stiffened and strained below her boned bodice.

'*Se thelo*...I want you,' Gio growled soft and low, ferocious tension etched in every taut athletic line of his lean, powerful body.

'*So much,*' she echoed in breathless agreement, her tummy performing a somersault as he ravaged her mouth in an electrifyingly passionate kiss.

As Leandros signalled to indicate his readiness to make a short speech and dealt him a highly amused smile, Gio set Billie back from him, shrewd eyes searching her bemused face. She was like a breath of fresh air in his life. Was that why she unsettled him? Tempted him into engaging in the kind of PDA he had never before indulged in? But then what other woman would have tolerated Calisto's appearance without throwing a big scene?

He watched Billie rise from her seat without hesitation to take Theo, who was stretching his arms out to her from a nearby table. Clearly tired and fed up, his son whimpered and clung to his mother like a little limpet before burying his head sleepily against her shoulder. Gio's rarely touched conscience was pierced by the sight when he thought of the iniquitous prenuptial agreement he had had drawn up to ensnare Billie. She was such an innocent. He had guessed that she wouldn't bother to read the terms, never mind the small print. Knowing she didn't give a damn about his money, he had taken ruthless advantage of her trusting nature....regardless of his awareness of how much she loved their son.

Of course, she need never know about the terms of the pre-nup, Gio reasoned, reckoning that he didn't want that coming back to haunt him at some inopportune time in the future. Billie would be shocked. Billie, who had always tried to see him as a nicer, kinder person than he could ever be, would for ever lose her rose-tinted view of him. He frowned, deciding that he would lose her copy of that document in a safe somewhere...

CHAPTER EIGHT

THE HELICOPTER LANDED in a clearing lit by torches on the island of Letsos.

'So, this is the island where you were born. Does it belong to you?' Billie remarked as Gio lifted her down to the ground and then went back to take Theo and assist the nanny in her descent.

'It still belongs to my grandfather, Theo's namesake. I imagine if it had ever passed to my father, it would've been sold long ago,' he opined drily. 'He sold everything that wasn't nailed down long before he died.'

'Did your family name the island after themselves?' she asked curiously.

'No, I believe my ancestors stole the name and began using it several generations back after a family dispute split them into two factions,' he explained, ushering her into the four-wheel-drive vehicle.

'I'm looking forward to meeting your family,' Billie lied because she felt she had to lie out of politeness.

While Billie was undeniably curious, she was also very apprehensive about the sort of reception she could expect to receive from Gio's wealthy relatives. In her own opinion she had so many strikes against her: the speed of their marriage, Theo's birth out of wedlock, never mind the reality that she was a complete stranger and a foreigner without either fancy lineage or cash. She was convinced that those facts would ensure that she was viewed with extreme suspicion and possibly even hostility.

'You'll meet them all tomorrow,' Gio told her calmly.

'But I assumed I'd be meeting them now...tonight,' she said tensely.

'It's been a very long day and we're not staying at the main house tonight. We'll introduce them to Theo in the morning.' Gio smoothed a hand down over Theo's back as his son squeezed out a cross little mutter as he secured him in a car seat. 'The sooner he's in bed, the better. Irene, you'll have the help of my old nursemaid tonight because I know you're tired. We're leaving Irene and Theo at Agata's house.'

'*Leaving*...Theo?' Billie parroted in dismay.

'Relax. It's not as though we're abandoning him on a park bench,' Gio censured with quiet amusement, dark eyes skimming her anxious face. 'We're spending our wedding night at the beach house. We'll pick up Theo in the morning before we go and meet the family. Agata will revel in being the first islander to get to know my son.'

When they drew up at Agata's house, Billie soon appreciated that Gio had not exaggerated because Theo's arrival was the source of much excitement and pleasure. Agata was middle-aged and rotund. She greeted Gio with overflowing affection and took hold of his son with a blissful smile while contriving simultaneously to offer Irene a warm welcome and the promise of a comfortable bed in her guest room.

Gio swept Billie back into the car. The road was soon travelling sharply downhill and the car finally stopped at the mouth of a sandy path. Their driver, a strapping youth, grabbed the heavy cases and trudged down the path, leaving them to follow.

'Watch your step. It's a steep track,' Gio warned, clamping a strong arm to her slender spine to steady her as her heels sank into the sandy surface.

'I'd never have worn these shoes if I'd realised we were going to a beach house!' Billie muttered ruefully. 'I'm dressed up in my fanciest togs because I thought I'd be meeting your family tonight.'

'I wanted to surprise you.'

'You've succeeded.' Billie laughed, staring down at the stretch of pristine beach coming into view as they descended. The sun had gone down but a brazier was burning, casting flickers of light across the sand and the dark waves washing into the cove.

The wooden beach house was tucked into a corner and lit up with fairy lights that looked like roses. 'Wow…that's *so* pretty!' Billie exclaimed, staring when she saw lights flickering beyond the floor-to-ceiling windows as well.

Gio carried her over the threshold and she lost one of her shoes and he said that was a good thing because she couldn't walk in them and she was smiling as he set her down on a polished wood floor. There were flowers everywhere she looked and lots of burning candles casting glimmers of moving light and shadow across the opulent interior. Their driver settled the cases in the adjoining bedroom and departed.

Billie wandered barefoot into the bedroom, appreciating the luxurious but plain furnishings and the wide, comfortable bed.

'Champagne?' Gio prompted.

'Maybe later. Right now, I want a shower more than anything,' she confided, keen to be free of the tailored dress and jacket she had worn to look smart. 'Could you unzip me?'

'If I unzip you,' Gio remarked as she shed her jacket and moved helpfully close, 'you'll never make it to the shower.'

The zip ran down. He spread the fabric back and pressed his mouth to the smooth slope of her shoulder. 'Your skin is so wondrously soft,' he told her huskily, skimming the short sleeves down her arms, giving the dress a helpful push downward as it threatened to settle at her waist, and lifting her out of the folds.

'I'm not going to get my shower,' Billie forecast as he turned her slowly round to face him.

'Well, possibly not until later and you might have to share it.' Gio grinned down at her, his eyes hot as the sun's rays on her exposed the lush curves of her figure in a green satin and lace bra and panties set. 'That's if I ever let you out of bed...'

Billie resisted a sudden urge to stupidly ask him if he thought her bottom was too large. She tried to stay a stable weight but she had never fussed about the curvy shape she had been born with, regarding that as a futile exercise destined to lead only to disappointment. Irritated by her sudden self-consciousness in his presence, she said instead, 'You're wearing way too many clothes.'

Gio hauled her up into his arms and kissed her with passionate force before bringing her down on the bed. 'A shower and food and civilised behaviour later...I promise,' he swore.

Billie's memory flew back to the many, many times in the past when Gio had barely stepped through the door of the apartment before grabbing her with the wild impatience and hunger she had always cherished in him, deeming that fervour proof that she was more important to him than he was ever likely to tell her. Of course, the fallout when he announced that he was marrying Calisto had been all the more painful to bear, she conceded ruefully. He had forced her to see the danger of wishful thinking, the foolishness of the assumptions that had made her feel secure. But as soon as she found herself thinking that way, Billie kicked out those negative thoughts and, reminding herself that this was their wedding night, she lay back on the bed where he had placed her.

Gio was her husband now and he was hers in so many ways that he had never been before, she conceded, trying to banish her worries. Together, she and Gio and Theo would be a family. They would also be part of a much bigger family, which she was praying would eventually accept her, even if it was only for Theo's sake.

'Who organised all this?' Billie asked, shifting a hand to indicate the flowers and the candles and the opulent comfort of the room's appointments. 'Is the beach house in regular use?'

'It hadn't been used in quite some time,' Gio admitted as he shed his shirt in a careless heap. 'Leandros' sister, Eva, is an interior designer and she agreed to do a rush job for me as a favour. She wasn't sure she would make the deadline until the last minute and only finished this afternoon. The household staff saw to the rest.'

'I love the candles and the flowers,' Billie admitted.

'I knew you would…you've always been such a romantic,' Gio teased.

'But you organised it so you must be a romantic too,' she pointed out, absolutely blown away by the gradually dawning realisation that Gio had had the beach house set up for their wedding night solely in an attempt to please her.

'I'll never be romantic,' he fielded wryly. 'But I am bright enough to work out what's required and deliver it, *glyka mou*.'

With the greatest difficulty, Billie dragged her attention from his washboard abs and the way his naturally golden skin sleekly delineated his ripcord musculature. He was gorgeous and yet he was with her and not with the equally gorgeous Calisto. For a split second she let that mystery unnerve her and then she squashed the thought flat, telling herself off for even thinking it. He was married to her now, *with* her, and Calisto was in the past. Gloriously unaware of her constant attacks of insecurity, Gio stepped out of his trousers and skimmed off his boxers in one fell swoop of impatience.

Her mouth ran dry, her heartbeat quickening. It had been so long since she had had the luxury of watching Gio strip. That day she had gone for lunch with him at his hotel and ended up in bed with him, he hadn't even got undressed. Her face burned at the recollection.

'What are you thinking about?' Gio breathed, stalking across the bedroom to join her on the bed.

And she told him and, surprisingly, he laughed. 'I wasn't exactly the cool seducer, was I? I was as hot for you as a teenage boy having sex for the first time but I did at least use a condom.'

'I got carried away too,' she soothed, running gentle fingers along his angular jaw line. 'But you'd best be careful. I'm not using any form of contraception.'

Gio tugged her down on the pillows beside him and leant over her. 'Do I need to be careful? I missed out on you being pregnant with Theo and I would be pretty excited if you were to conceive again,' he admitted, dark eyes shimmering gold in the candlelight.

That was the most confidence-boosting thing Gio could have said to her, Billie reflected dizzily. His interest in her having a second child took her by storm because it meant that he regarded their marriage as a long-term venture rather than an exercise to simply grant Theo his legal birthright.

'I put on a lot of weight when I'm pregnant,' she warned him.

'And in all the best places,' Gio husked, running an admiring finger across a bra cup overflowing with soft creamy flesh. '*Theos*, I *love* your body.'

'Honestly?' Billie prompted, loathing herself for pressing the point.

'I can't keep my hands off you, Billie,' Gio groaned, flipping open the catch on her bra and filling his hands with the bounty he had been admiring. 'I never could…'

Her wretched brain was still shooting in directions she didn't want it to. It was urging her to ask why he had then chosen to marry a woman like Calisto and suddenly she couldn't restrain that need to know any longer and she asked, 'Then why did you marry a woman half my size?'

There was a sudden deathly silence. His head bent while he toyed with the warm soft curves he had bared, Gio glanced up at her from below his ridiculously long lashes. 'For all the *wrong* reasons…and I paid the price,' he admitted in a roughened undertone.

Billie wanted to dig deeper into the topic but she also knew that she didn't want to spoil their wedding night with the shadow of past pain and loss. With an almighty effort she cleared her head of such morbid reflections and said nothing at all because regret had coloured every syllable he spoke. Regret was enough to satisfy her, wasn't it? How much of a pint of blood did she need to satisfy her damaged ego? Enough blood to cause ructions in their shiny new marriage when Gio had already mentioned a desire for another child? She thought not, decided it was better to leave the past where it belonged and look to a brighter future.

Gio captured a turgid nipple in his mouth and toyed with it until it was throbbing. Billie rested back, letting the heat flow through her, warming and moistening ever more sensitive parts. Her hips shifted, her fingers raked through his short hair, eyes sliding shut as she held him to her with a deep sense of happiness. Another baby? What a sign of optimism on his part! He was a child of a broken marriage and she was convinced he would not risk bringing a second child into the mix if he believed their relationship was likely to break down.

'Tomorrow's going to come too soon for me,' Gio complained huskily as he tugged up her knees and peeled down her knickers in one smooth operation. 'But if I make love to you all night, you'll be too tired to meet my family in the morning.'

'You've got every night with me that you want now,' Billie whispered as he shifted to trace the moist cleft between her legs with a roving forefinger and she quivered instantaneously, every tingling nerve ending instantly clamouring for more.

'And I'm going to make the most of every opportunity. I'm sex-starved,' Gio confided, working a trail of lusty nipping and sucking across the upper slope of her breasts to her throat. 'I never could get enough of you. Now I've finally got you round the clock, I'll be very demanding.'

'Promises…promises,' Billie quipped, warmed by that threat, for the more Gio expressed his desire for her, the more secure she felt.

As excitement began to claim Billie, conversation died because she couldn't think straight for long enough to vocalise. He touched her with the unerring skill of an expert and she writhed, hands digging into his cropped black hair as he used his mouth to bring her to a shattering climax.

Weak with satiation in the aftermath, she loosed a startled gasp as Gio flipped her over onto her stomach. 'What—?'

'I'm in a very dominant mood, *moro mou*,' Gio growled, gripping her hips and driving hard into her passion-moistened depths, stretching her to the limit with his length and girth and sending a renewed and arousing wash of hunger through her.

And Billie had always secretly liked it when Gio was forcefully passionate in bed. Then as now, his dominance somehow made her feel irresistible. A helpless shudder of response snaked through her quivering body, her breath rasping in her throat, her heart hammering as he plunged into her with pounding erotic urgency. It went on and on and on, igniting the bittersweet torment of need inside her again. A carnal finger stroked and encircled her clitoris and the tightening knot of tension in her womb started up a chain reaction. A string of tiny inner convulsions pulsed along her inner channel and finally merged into a rapturous explosion of soul-destroying pleasure.

'That's something you're very, very good at,' Billie mumbled unsteadily just as Gio began to pull away from her and she grabbed his arm, eyes flying wide in the candlelight. 'No, don't, *don't* move away. I hate it when you do that.'

'It's just the way I am,' Gio framed, frowning.

Billie brought up another hand to grip his shoulder. 'But it doesn't have to be like that. You can hug Theo.'

'That's different.'

Billie knew she was hitting barriers and that possibly she hadn't chosen the best time to complain, but his habit of shifting away from all contact in the immediate aftermath of intimacy had always hurt her feelings. 'You've never had a problem with hugging me if I'm upset about anything, have you?'

'Well, no, *but*—'

'So, pretend I'm upset,' Billie urged with all the enthusiasm of a woman who believed she had found the perfect solution to his lack in the affection department.

Gio settled dazed eyes on her. *'What?'* he breathed in disbelief.

'After sex,' Billie told him bluntly. 'Just think. She's upset, now I have to hug her.'

'I don't want to think of you being *upset* after we make love.'

'Have you got an argument against absolutely everything?' Billie asked him in a pained tone. 'I was trying to work out a strategy which would suit us both.'

'Forget the strategy,' Gio advised, anchoring both arms firmly round her and hauling her back against him with gritted teeth. 'I'll work on it…OK?'

'OK,' Billie agreed, satisfied, running an exploring hand down over his hair-roughened torso and then teasingly lower in an operation destined to prove to him there would be advantages to a change of behaviour that brought him physically closer.

'OK,' Gio said again but in a deep husky purr. '*Very* OK…'

An hour later they were outdoors, lying relaxed on the huge upholstered recliner on the deck and watching the flames from the brazier shooting up against the night sky. Discarded dishes from the packed fridge were scattered around, evidence of the substantial meal they had contrived to eat. Billie laced her fingers round the stem of her champagne flute and heaved a contented sigh. 'It's incredibly peaceful here with just the sound of the sea in the background.'

'I always loved that sound when I was a kid. My parents used to bring us down here and…' Gio's voice trailed away into silence.

Billie glanced up at him, aware of the tension now stiffening his long, lean length against her. 'And… *what*?' she pressed. 'It's great that you've got some good memories of your childhood.'

'My sisters and I were very young then. It was long before my parents broke up…before my father met *the love of his life.*' Gio voiced that emphasis with biting derision.

'Oh…and she was?' Billie jumped straight into the opening he had given her because he had always avoided the subject of his parents' divorce.

'An English fashion model called Marianne. She was his mistress and when she became *accidentally* pregnant—with the boy who later turned out not to be my father's—he decided that he couldn't live without her.'

'Oh,' Billie said in quite another tone, discomfited by the similarities she saw to their own previous relationship, wondering if she was at last learning the reason why Gio had always maintained an emotional distance in their relationship.

'My sisters and I returned from boarding school for our summer break and learned that our whole lives had changed. My father had divorced my mother and stuck her in an Athens apartment. Suddenly we weren't welcome on Letsos or in our childhood home any more because my father—and it is a challenge to compliment him with that label—had married Marianne and she refused to have the children of his first marriage hanging around.'

The depth of Gio's bitterness shocked Billie but she could imagine how horrible it must have been for him and his sisters to see their mother rejected and all of them excluded from everything they had become accustomed to believing was theirs. 'Didn't your grandfather intervene? You said he owned this island.'

'He couldn't disown his son though, and naturally

he didn't want to make an enemy of his new daughter-in-law. He does regret, however, that he didn't do more to help my mother, but at the time he was really struggling to repair the damage Dmitri's extravagance and marriage breakdown had already done to the family and the business.'

'Did you have much contact with your father after the divorce?' Billie asked.

'No, after that one meeting, I only saw him one more time. Marianne very much resented the fact that he had had other children. Love,' Gio breathed witheringly, 'can be a very destructive emotion. My father destroyed his family in the name of love and my mother never recovered from the treatment she suffered at his hands.'

Billie was thoughtful because she was finally seeing when Gio had reached the conclusion that the softer human emotions could be toxic. As a child, Gio had seen the consequences of what he believed to be love in all its selfish, dangerous glory when his father had sacrificed his family so that he could be with the woman he wanted.

'You can't say that a parent's love for their child is destructive,' she commented mildly. 'Most people see it as supportive.'

'A man of principle can do what he should do for his family without prating about love,' Gio asserted with a slight shudder as he tightened his arms round her. 'I don't need to love you to look after you.'

Billie's eyes stung painfully. He, most certainly, hadn't been looking after her when he had chosen to marry Calisto two years earlier but that was not a memory she wished to rouse. Instead she set down her glass and pillowed her head against his shoulder.

'I suppose,' Gio said, after a great deal of unusually introspective thought, 'I do love Theo but it's because he's little and helpless. He's got all the appeal of a puppy or a kitten. I took dozens of photos of him on my phone before I left Yorkshire and I couldn't wait to see him again.'

Billie thought it was sad that at that moment she envied her son for having that amount of pull with Gio after such a short acquaintance.

'I couldn't wait to see you either…as you know when I turned up today before you could even make it to the church,' Gio confided, nuzzling his unshaven jaw line softly along the line of her creamy throat, feeling extraordinarily at peace for the first time in a very long time and wondering what it was about her that had that effect on him. 'I don't know why I did that. It was absolutely crazy.'

'I didn't mind,' Billie interposed, squirming round in the circle of his arms to look down at him instead of up at the stars.

His lean, strong face was still a touch bemused by his own behaviour that morning and it was obvious that he was still mulling that over. 'You know, somewhere in the back of my mind, I honestly think I was afraid you mightn't turn up at the church… Isn't that insane?'

If he had known how much she loved him, he would have known he was quite safe on that score, she reflected ruefully. No, no matter how mad she had been with him she would never have jilted him at the altar.

'My goodness, it's a huge house,' Billie breathed as the four-wheel drive parked outside a very large sprawling villa set high on the hillside and surrounded by glorious tropical gardens.

'It has to be big for family get-togethers and it's been extended by almost every generation since it was built.' His tension pronounced enough to attract Billie's notice, Gio sprang out and turned back to un-strap Theo from the car seat while Irene and Agata headed up the wide, shallow steps that led to a front door that already stood wide.

The housekeeper hovering at the door fussed around them but Gio would not even linger long enough to perform an introduction and strode on past, knowing exactly where he was going and clearly de-termined not to be held back.

'Gio!' Billie exclaimed, hurrying out of breath in his wake. 'If we're going into a crowd, give me Theo. He can be awkward with strangers...'

His stubborn jaw line clenching, Gio passed their son to Billie, who settled the toddler comfortably on her hip. 'And smile, for goodness' sake,' she urged, troubled by the forbidding cast of his lean, darkly handsome features. 'It doesn't matter if your fam-ily aren't too sure about me...you have to give them time...'

The elegant reception room was in proportion with

the house and very big and Billie was disconcerted to peer in the glass doors and see an absolute throng of people, both standing and seated, on the marble floor. Gio had a much bigger family than she had appreciated. As they entered the room every head turned towards them and Billie sucked in her tummy by breathing in deep and slow, striving to steady her nerves.

'I asked you all here today to introduce you to my wife,' Gio declared in the rushing silence, his dark deep drawl measured and carrying to every corner of the room. 'This is Billie. We got married yesterday and—'

A noise erupted from the far corner as an older man stood up and banged his walking cane loudly on the floor. His lined face rigid, he shot a stream of furious Greek at Gio. Gio grated something back and then closed an arm to Billie's spine to thrust her back in the direction of the door. 'We are leaving,' he said curtly.

'Oh, please, don't go, Gio!' A tall, shapely brunette was chasing after them. 'I'm Sofia, Gio's youngest sister. Gio, why on earth didn't you tell us that you were getting married?'

Billie stopped dead and swopped Theo to her other hip because he was getting heavy. 'He *didn't* tell any of you?' She gasped in disbelief.

'No, he said he had a surprise to share with us and that's why we're all here.'

'We're leaving, Billie,' Gio reminded her doggedly. But Billie spun round before he could open the door and marched back into the room. 'Gio should have told you that we were getting married. I had no idea—'

'Billie,' Gio cut in, clamping an imprisoning hand to her shoulder.

'Well, I'm sorry to criticise you in front of your family but you really should have warned them. Obviously everybody's in shock and people say things they don't necessarily mean when you shock them,' Billie pointed out, studying the fuming older man, who she suspected was Gio's grandfather, Theon Letsos. 'There's no sense in storming out in a huff over it.'

'I am not in a huff,' Gio ground out between clenched teeth, outraged that she was defying his lead and his wishes with his own family.

'Perhaps we could talk about this,' the old man said gruffly, scanning Billie with astute dark eyes that reminded her strongly of Gio's. 'Your wife is correct. I spoke in haste and without thought.'

'He insulted you,' Gio bit out harshly.

'That's all right. I can only be offended if you abuse me in English,' Billie declared forgivingly. 'I don't speak a word of Greek!'

'Gio and his sisters attended English schools,' the older man told her with a sudden smile. 'Now come and sit down and tell me about yourself. I find it hard to stand for long.'

In a state of disbelief, Gio found himself in the rare position of being assigned second string within his family as Billie, chattering away to his grandfather as though she had known him for years rather than seconds, walked slowly over to the closest seats available.

'Forgive me for being so remiss in the courtesies,' Theon murmured. 'I am Gio's grandfather, Theon Letsos.'

'I'm Billie. It's not short for anything.'

'And your son?'

'*Our* son,' Gio corrected with pride. 'Theon Giorgios, your great-grandson, known as Theo.'

Taken aback by the revelation, the older man studied Theo as he crawled across the floor with all the energy of a toddler kept in restraint for too long. 'Theo...' he mused in the crashing silence that had once again engulfed the entire room. 'And you only married *yesterday*?'

'Gio only found out that Theo existed very recently,' Billie cut in hastily. 'We hadn't been in contact for a couple of years—'

Gio gritted his teeth. 'There is absolutely no need for you to talk about that.'

'Of course there is. I don't want anyone thinking that I had an on-going affair with a married man,' Billie declared without hesitation, marvelling at how slow on the uptake Gio could sometimes be because *he* was totally indifferent to what other people thought of him. But she didn't want that stigma within the family circle. She might not have liked Calisto, nonetheless she would not have engaged in a relationship with Gio with or without his wife's knowledge.

'A great-grandson named for me...' Theon was keen to concentrate on the positive and politely ignore Gio's brooding protective stance beside Billie's chair. 'A fine boy…not shy either!' he remarked with an appreciative laugh as Theo made his way over to another toddler with a small heap of toys in front of him and snatched at the first colourful item he could reach.

'So, tell me about yourself,' the older man invited.

'Billie's not here for an interview,' Gio incised coolly.

'My goodness, I'm *so* thirsty. I would really love a drink,' Billie informed Gio, shooting him an expectant look.

Of course, Gio simply snapped his fingers like some desert potentate and a uniformed maid materialised.

Billie met Theon's amused eyes and her own mouth twitched because her strategy had been lame but she really could have done without Gio standing over her in warrior mode as if she were defenceless in enemy territory. He had never acted that way around her before and the discovery that his reserve was as great within his own family as it had once been with her was a major shock to her expectations. Yet that insight saddened her as well. Gio was such a lone wolf. How had he contrived to become the guarded, unemotional male he was with such a large and, she sensed, loving family?

Theo crawled back and hauled himself up against Billie's knees and then clutched at his father's legs until Gio abandoned his rigid stance, smiled with a sudden brilliance that lit up his lean, strong face and swept his son up in his arms to carry him back to the toys.

'It's been a long time since I saw Gio smile,' Theon remarked.

'I don't have a fancy background or any money. I owned and ran a shop. I'm just an ordinary working woman,' Billie volunteered before Gio could return to censor the conversation. 'You might as well know that upfront.'

'In recent years, *very* recent years, I have learned the unimportance of such distinctions.' Theon gave an emphatic shrug and relaxed back into his armchair. 'And I'm afraid I must disagree with you on one point. No ordinary woman could handle Gio and the Letsos family with so much tolerance and common sense.'

That was Billie's last private moment with Theon. One by one she received introductions to Gio's uncles, aunts and sisters, including, to her surprise, his half-sister, Melissa, who had passed half a lifetime being royally ignored by her father's family because she was the result of Dmitri Letsos' illicit teenaged romance.

'They're not a bad bunch when you get to know them,' Melissa, a collected blonde teacher in her forties, pronounced with a wry smile. 'Oh, there's the usual sibling rivalry, but they are, one and all—I assure you—devoted to Gio. He brought me into this family and he's the first port of call for all of us when there's a crisis. I hope you can handle that. Calisto couldn't.'

From stray comments made and generally quickly leading to a subject change rather than risk causing

offence, Billie began to suspect that Gio's first wife
had not been well liked. She cursed her own curiosity
about her predecessor: it was pointless and the grati-
fication of that curiosity was more likely to lead to
hurt. Gio had married another woman. *Get over it*,
she urged herself impatiently, determined not to be
haunted by the shadows of the past.

'If your wife is the woman she appears to be,
she's solid gold,' Gio's grandfather told him disconcertingly.

Tight-mouthed, Gio breathed, 'When it comes to
Billie, I have no need of anyone's approval.'

'But an invitation to the wedding would have been
very much appreciated,' Theon countered drily.

Once Irene had taken Theo up for his bath and
guests had begun to disperse to their own corners of
the rambling villa, Billie slipped away to explore the
wonderful gardens, finally sitting down in the shade
of an ancient chestnut tree to appreciate the glorious
bird's-eye view of the island and the ocean. Although
she was exhausted she was quietly pleased that her
meeting with Gio's family had ultimately gone well
when it had so very nearly gone badly wrong.

When had Gio become so hot-tempered? He had
been like a stick of dynamite with a smouldering
string attached, aggressively ready to attack anyone
who attacked her, over-sensitive to every comment
and question that came in her direction. Billie sighed
over that mystery and slowly relaxed, letting the tension drain out of her.

'I've been looking everywhere for you,' Gio delivered in a minatory tone, striding down the gravelled path towards her. 'Downstairs, upstairs...'

'Maybe you should microchip me and then you would know where I am at all times,' Billie told him deadpan.

Struggling to master his exasperation, Gio released his breath in a rush. There she was, curls foaming round her lovely face, eyes contemplative, clearly happy and content. He could not explain to her his personal fear that she had put on a fantastic sociable act all day for the benefit of his family while secretly masking her hurt at her less than welcoming reception. 'Are you all right?'

'Tired,' she admitted, sleepy green eyes locked to him while a wicked little current of remembered pleasure travelled through her. 'But then we didn't get much sleep last night...'

The faintest colour stung his stunning cheekbones, brilliant dark eyes flaring gold, lean bronzed features breathtaking in their perfect symmetry as his wide mouth took on a sensual curve. She loved him; she loved him so much, she acknowledged helplessly.

'What are you out here worrying about?'

'I'm not worrying,' Billie declared. 'This is a gorgeous garden and I'm enjoying it.'

Recalling the window boxes and pot plants she used to keep at the apartment, Gio felt his conscience ping. Just as quickly he recalled the hollow sensation he had suffered when, following her disappearance, he had seen those plants dead and withered and as always he buried the memory deep of that period in his life. 'I should've bought you a house with a garden a long time ago.'

'My only experience of gardening was visiting my granddad's allotment as a child,' Billie confided quietly. 'He used to plant vegetable seeds for me. That was in the days before the betting shop and the drink pushed him into a less active lifestyle.'

Gio frowned, astonished by the sudden realisation that he could know so little about his wife's background. Momentarily he marvelled that he had never asked her anything beyond the most basic questions, but, after learning that she had virtually no living relatives that she knew of, he had seen no reason to probe deeper. 'He was a drunk?'

'No, that's too harsh. He drank to escape my grandma's nagging. She was kind of sour in nature. If he was a drunk,' Billie extended, 'he was a nice drunk because he was never mean, but his liver failed and he was ill for a long time. That's when I first began missing school because my grandma wouldn't look after him the way he needed to be looked after and I felt so guilty leaving him to her care every day.'

'Surely there was some care offered by the state?'

'No, there's actually very little help available. Grandma was told he wasn't sick enough to get a bed in a nursing home even though he was terminally ill. Once he had passed, it was just her and me... and she never liked me, said I reminded her of my mother.' Billie grimaced. 'You can't really blame her. My mother dumped me on her and never came back. She was a bitter woman, who just never saw the good in anyone. I got to go back to school for a couple of years and then Grandma's health failed too and that was the end of that.'

Gio was stunned by what he was belatedly learning. 'How is it that I'm only finding out all this about you now?' he could not help asking, as if he thought the oversight might somehow be her fault.

Tactfully concealing her wonder at that question, Billie shot him a wry glance. 'Gio, back then, in your eyes, when I wasn't physically in front of you, I didn't exist.'

Gio tensed. 'That's untrue.'

'Do you recall that cabinet with drawers I once mentioned where I was tucked in my own tiny drawer, only to be taken out and appreciated by you on special occasions? Seriously, I wasn't joking—that *was* what it was like.'

His lean dark features were grim. 'What you're really saying is that I'm a colossally selfish individual.'

'You were self-absorbed and very driven. Let's face it, when we were together your main focus was always business. I also think you were too posh to be comfortable with the difference in our backgrounds. Ignoring it was easier. I think as long as I was willing to be quiet about it, you preferred not to be reminded that I was once a humble cleaner,' Billie told him gently.

'I can't believe we're even having this conversation!' Gio ground out angrily, his temper, kept on a short leash all day, whipping up in a sudden surge hotter than lava. 'Or that you could ever have had such a low opinion of me!'

In mute frustration, Billie closed her eyes and counted to ten. 'It's done and dusted, Gio—it's the past. I'm not attacking you. I'm only being honest. I wasn't perfect either. I should have stood up to you, demanded more, but I was too young and in my very first relationship.'

'You lied about your age.' Gio was quick to pounce on that reminder.

Billie nodded peaceably, refusing to rise to the bait because there was no way she was about to engage in a massive row with Gio about their past. After all, everything had changed now and they were making a new start at a very different level of intimacy.

'I've got some work to do,' Gio said in a tone of finality.

Billie smiled, knowing his first refuge when emotion threatened was work. 'I'll walk back indoors with you.'

Gio settled with his laptop in the library, which was set up like a high-tech office for his use. *Theos*, he still found himself thinking furiously, he was not and he never had been a selfish person. On one issue, Billie was correct: he had no need whatsoever to revisit the past. That conviction in place, Gio struggled to concentrate on the lines of figures on his laptop screen and he was fine until the moment that the matter of the pre-nuptial settlement contract squeezed into his mind and practically obliterated everything else in the process. He rang the housekeeper to discover where Billie's possessions had been stored since being shipped out the previous week.

It occurred to him then without warning that even the devil could not have devised a more colossally selfish or fiendish document. He refused to act like a male engaged in a covert operation, but on some level of his brain he was astounded by what he was about to do when he finally stood in the room confronted with a heap of boxes. After all, when was Billie ever likely to lift that contract out and reread it? Why the hell was he so damned rattled by a very minor risk? Perspiration dampened his lean, bronzed features. He was engaging in a cover-up and the knowledge didn't sit well with him. But prior to that contract he had never once been dishonest with Billie. He hovered, studying the boxes. That document could *hurt* her, he reflected broodingly, and he latched onto that excuse for what he was about to do with alacrity.

Gio had never unpacked a box in his life but he wasn't surprised by the discovery that every box was labelled and incredibly neatly filled because Billie was very, very organised and always had been. In the third box, he hit the pay dirt of finding files full of papers and in the second file he espied the contract and ripped it out, but not before he frowned down at a certificate for wine tasting and found beneath it one for art appreciation. He went through the whole file, checking the dates, learning what he knew he should have learned years sooner.

There was a burning behind his eyes that made them feel scratchy and he felt oddly hollow, as though someone had gutted him without warning. Feeling rather as though he had been beaten up, Gio replaced everything where he had found it with the exception of the contract and strode off to pour himself a very stiff drink. The contract went through the shredder but the relief he had expected to feel was utterly absent. He had gone digging where he had no business digging, he conceded sardonically, and he rather thought that in the process he had got what he deserved.

'Theon wants you to join him for afternoon tea,' Sofia told Billie cheerfully around three that afternoon. 'It's a big honour.'

Billie grinned. 'I liked him.'

'I think the feeling's reciprocated,' Gio's sister responded with a laugh as she guided Billie across the villa to the wing of the house Theon occupied.

A manservant showed her out onto a big shaded balcony where Theon awaited her. 'I believe this is an honour,' Billie remarked with a grin.

'How on earth have you escaped Gio?' his grandfather enquired mockingly.

'Something I said annoyed him… He's taken refuge in work,' Billie confided, marvelling at how very comfortable she felt in the older man's company.

'I overheard that conversation,' Theon admitted, disconcerting her. 'This balcony is directly overhead.'

Billie reddened but sat down. 'Oh, well, it's all within the family,' she said without great concern because it wasn't as if she and Gio had been hurling insults at each other or discussing anything she considered particularly private, although she knew that put in the same position Gio would have been furious.

'I thought I should bring you up to date on some family history, as I doubt very much that Gio has done the job for me,' Theon commented.

'I know about his parents' divorce,' Billie contributed. 'And I know his father really didn't have much to do with him after it.'

'Dmitri was a weak man. There, I have said it,' the older man said wryly. 'For years I wouldn't admit that to myself because he was my son...'

'It's challenging to accept faults in those we care about most,' Billie murmured soothingly.

'You love Gio a great deal—it shines from you,' his grandfather told her. 'He's a very lucky man.'

Billie flushed and decided not to embarrass herself with a denial while she poured the tea. 'I hope he always thinks so. He's much more complicated than I am...'

'And that's why I invited you for tea,' Theon told her. 'I'm very much afraid that his complexity can be laid at my door. I raised Gio from the age of eleven after his mother died.'

'I had no idea she died while he was still so young,' Billie said in surprise as she buttered a scone and deliberated with some gastronomic anticipation on whether to have raspberry or strawberry jam with her cream.

'Ianthe couldn't cope alone after Dmitri divorced her for Marianne. I had no idea how bad things had become for Gio's mother,' Theon told her heavily.

'Perhaps if my wife had still been alive she would have had the wisdom to foresee the problems and she would have encouraged me to offer help in time to prevent a tragedy.'

Billie set down her scone after one delicious bite. 'A tragedy?' she pressed.

'Ianthe hanged herself…and Gio found her,' the older man recounted with a shudder. 'I will carry the burden of my guilt to the end of my days.'

Eyes widening, Billie had lost colour. 'I had no idea…'

'I didn't think you would, which is why I told you,' Gio's grandfather confessed. 'The effect on Gio was catastrophic. He had lost his father, his home and then his mother, only a few months later.'

Billie shook her head slowly, cringing at the thought of such a huge loss being inflicted on Gio and his sisters while they were still so young. 'That must have been dreadful for him,' she muttered unsteadily, her heart swelling. 'He would've felt responsible—'

'I worried that Gio would inherit the same excessively emotional personality that both Dmitri and Ianthe demonstrated in the way they led their lives. That kind of emotional intensity leads to instability.'

'Not always,' Billie inserted gently.

Theon shook his white head. 'I wanted to be sure that Gio did not repeat his father's mistakes. It was too much responsibility to place on a child's shoulders. In many ways I taught him the wrong values,' he explained with unashamed guilt etched in his lined features. 'I expected, *wanted* him to marry well…

and we all know how successful that proved to be. I put far too much emphasis on wealth, status and family duty—'

'But,' Billie cut in with an apologetic look, 'at the end of the day, Gio is a highly intelligent adult and totally independent and he made his own decisions.'

'*Ne*…yes, and he married you without telling any of us because he refused even to risk the fact that I might have tried to interfere.'

'Probably,' Billie agreed thoughtfully. 'But he's not enough in touch with his own feelings to even know that.'

'You know him so well,' Theon pronounced with appreciation. 'Now we've got the difficult bit over, shall we enjoy our scones?'

Gio was on the phone to Leandros and Leandros was asking awkward questions, destined not to be answered. 'I just don't understand.' His best friend sighed. 'You only got married yesterday. You only arrived with your family today. Why would you want to fly back to Athens for one night simply to have some fancy dinner?'

'Tomorrow's Billie's birthday.'

'So, make it tomorrow, then.'

'I want to do it tonight. Are you joining us?' Gio prompted. 'And, Leandros, if you mention Canaletto, I'll cut your throat.'

'Of course I'll join you.'

Billie was engaged in drying Theo and slotting

him into his pyjamas when Gio appeared in the bathroom doorway of the nursery suite.

Gio swept up his son and hugged him and did the flying thing again, which sent Theo into gales of laughter. 'He's tired,' Gio acknowledged as Theo then rested his curly head down on his father's shoulder and slumped.

'He's had a lot of excitement today and he's always exhausted when he's been with other kids.' Billie carried her son through to the bedroom and settled him down in the very fancy cot, from which she quickly detached the flouncy hangings and everything else within reach for such dangling temptations were not a good idea with an active toddler.

'This place needs to be refurnished,' Gio commented tautly, watching her every move, it seemed, unsettling her.

Billie laughed. 'It's perfectly fine. It might have been done up for a little girl but Theo doesn't know the difference yet.'

'It was decorated for Sofia's youngest daughter. She had a difficult birth and her husband was travelling and Theon suggested she move back here while he was away,' Gio volunteered.

'Sofia's lovely,' Billie said warmly.

'We're going out tonight,' Gio announced abruptly.

'Where to?'

'Athens.'

Billie blinked. '*Athens*? But we've only just got here!'

'We'll be back tomorrow,' Gio sliced in. 'We're eating out with Leandros and his current girlfriend.'

'Are they getting engaged or something?'

'Not that I know of. Is going out with me such a big deal?' Gio demanded in frustration.

Billie almost said that, naturally, it was a big deal when he had never taken her anywhere public in years, aside of the wedding, but she thought better of that piece of one-upmanship. She was reluctant to hark back to the past when their marriage was, self-evidently, a very new and much altered situation. She supposed that, for Gio, taking a flight for one night out was almost normal, certainly nothing he appeared to have to think about, and she resolved to say no more while privately worrying about what she had to wear.

She blessed the foresight that had sent her out shopping for more sophisticated and expensive clothes before the wedding and pulled an elegant pewter-coloured dress from a closet in the luxurious dressing room where all her clothes had been carefully unpacked for her. While she showered and attended to renewing her make-up, she pondered Gio's strange mood.

'What do you think?' she asked, twirling a little apprehensively in front of him when she found him waiting in the bedroom for her.

Stunning dark golden eyes flared over her. 'You look incredible,' he intoned with convincing appreciation. 'Are you ready to leave?'

A warm sense of acceptance blossomed inside Billie even though she could still not understand how he could have been married to a beauty like Calisto and still deem his infinitely less-beautiful second wife equal to the label 'incredible'.

'Are we returning to Letsos tonight?' she prompted as she let Gio lift her into the helicopter.

'Yes, although the family own a city apartment if you would prefer to stay there,' he volunteered.

'No, I'd miss Theo at breakfast time when he's all warm and cuddly and glad to see me,' Billie confided sunnily.

As the helicopter rose in the air Gio leant closer, meshing long fingers into the tumble of her curls. He turned her face up and crushed her mouth under his in a breathtakingly hot kiss and that not only startled her, but also sent hunger crashing greedily through her body.

Billie rested disconcerted eyes on him in the aftermath. His lean, darkly beautiful face was slashed by a brilliant smile and he closed one hand firmly over hers. Wonderment filtered through Billie. There was something wrong but she didn't know what it was...

CHAPTER NINE

BILLIE WALKED INTO the upmarket art gallery with one hand resting on Gio's arm. The owner swam up to them wreathed in smiles. Wine was served while they were treated to a personalised tour of the exhibits. Billie was bored but worked hard not to show it, politely absorbing the pretentious descriptions of canvases that looked as though a toddler had thrown paint at them.

'Do you see anything you like?' Gio enquired, apparently surprised by his wife's unresponsive silence.

'I'm not an art buff. I sort of prefer more traditional paintings,' she whispered back guiltily, and then she stiffened, staring across the gallery at the unmistakeable figure of Calisto, sheathed in a scarlet minidress and virtually impossible to miss.

'What the hell…?' Gio breathed irritably above her head.

'I'll deal with this,' Billie announced, startling him, walking across the marble tiles with her wine glass clasped in one determined hand.

'How did you know we were going to be here?' Billie asked Gio's ex-wife without hesitation.

Calisto's ice-blue eyes glinted. 'I have my sources, but aren't you a little out of your depth in this milieu?'

'I believe you're the one out of your depth. Gio isn't coming back to you,' Billie responded stiffly. 'This is a waste of your time.'

'Oh, I don't think so. Once I heard the terms of your pre-nup, I knew you would be on your way out almost as soon as you arrived,' Calisto trilled with a scornful smirk. 'You signed it without reading it, didn't you? Silly, silly woman. Remember that when Gio dumps you back in the UK *without* your precious son!'

Billie refused to react in any way, determined not to give Calisto that much satisfaction. The woman hated her: she could see that. It was there in the dripping malevolence of her gaze and the sneering tone of her voice and Billie was challenged to understand what exactly she had done to incite such intense loathing. Simply marrying Gio? Her custody of Gio's son? Or was Calisto still in love with Gio and feeling scorned by his rapid remarriage?

Gio strolled up and without a word to even acknowledge his ex-wife walked Billie out of the gallery. 'Only two people knew we were coming here and one of them is Damon, whom I trust with my life,' he told her grimly. 'I've already called him. He will deal with the leak and the person concerned will be sacked.'

'I think that would be best,' Billie said rather woodenly. 'And perhaps the lawyer, whom you men-

tioned is her stepbrother? He seems to have talked out
of turn about confidential matters as well.'

Gio frowned, making it obvious that he had not
overheard Calisto's final salvo. 'What confidential
matters?'

Billie shrugged as though she meant something
trivial, reluctant to think the worst of Gio, averse to
trusting anything that witch, Calisto, had claimed
at his expense. She would dig out the pre-nup and
check it out for herself or arrange to have it looked
over by an independent lawyer. It couldn't be true; it
couldn't possibly be true, she thought in an agony of
fear. After all, if that claim of Calisto's was true, it
would mean that their marriage was an empty cha-
rade, never intended to do anything but gain Gio
legal custody of Theo and she could not, *would* not
believe that of him!

'Your ex is a bit of a pyscho,' Billie remarked ten-
tatively as they settled into the waiting limousine.

'And probably what I deserved,' Gio breathed in
a raw undertone of stress.

'What's the matter with you?' Billie prompted before they entered the fashionable restaurant.

'Nothing's the matter,' Gio insisted.

If you can believe that, you can believe anything,
Billie reflected, unimpressed, off-balanced by the odd
way he was behaving. He was still holding her hand,
still acting as if he were physically welded to her or,
ridiculously, as though he were afraid that she might
run away somewhere.

No way, Billie thought combatively. He had signed

up for a life sentence as far as she was concerned and he was going to serve it, she thought crazily, studying his lean, bronzed, totally gorgeous profile while he talked to Leandros and Billie listened to Leandros' girlfriend, Claire, who was a British model, talk about the joys of fake tan and the cosmetics range she was planning. It wasn't riveting stuff but Billie tried her best to be friendly while reaching the conclusion that Leandros was as shallow as a puddle when it came to the female sex.

Gio skated a teasing forefinger along Billie's thigh below the table and she tensed, thinking, not about what he probably hoped she was thinking about, but instead about what Calisto had said. I'm going to have to ask him, she accepted unhappily.

Was he capable of such a deception through the means of a legal document? Oh, yes, Billie had no doubts when it came to how ruthless Gio could be. After all, in spite of what she had deemed to be a very happy relationship and her warning that she would not be there when he returned, Gio had still gone off and married another woman because that was what he'd felt he *had* to do. Like a granite rock rolling down a hill on a set path, Gio was not given to second thoughts or doubts or insecurities like frailer personalities and he didn't think much about the damage he could be inflicting.

How could she love someone like that? Billie asked herself wretchedly as the limousine carried them back to the airport.

'What did you think of Claire?' Gio enquired in

the silence, desperate to know what Calisto had said to her. Calisto could be so vicious and, when she aimed it at Billie, even Gio was willing to admit that she had some excuse for her resentment.

'Very chatty and glam. She seems pleasant enough,' Billie commented.

'For a fake-tan expert. She must be great in bed,' Gio said sardonically.

'Why?' Billie heard herself say. 'Is that how you first thought about me? Let's face it, I didn't have much in the way of intellectual conversation to offer either.'

'We're not talking about you.' Gio gave her hand a little shake as though in rebuke. 'You were never that vain or frivolous.'

'Claire's looks are the basis of her whole career so I don't think it's fair to call her vain or frivolous.' And in the back of her mind, Billie was wondering why she was arguing with him about something that didn't matter in the slightest to her. Dimly it dawned on her that fear was working on her nerves, cutting through the sense of trust and security that she had begun to develop and throwing up friction in her every response to him.

What on earth was she planning to do if the man she loved turned out to be her worst enemy rather than her husband? How was she going to cope with Gio trying to take Theo away from her? Murder him in his bed? Hire a hit man? Her mind threw up crazier and crazier ideas and her tension rose steadily as she boarded the helicopter to sit stiff and silent by his side until the flight back to Letsos was complete.

'I wish you'd tell me what's wrong,' Gio breathed as she pulled away from his supporting arm and picked an uneven passage along the path from the helipad to the villa.

'We'll talk about it inside where nobody can hear us,' Billie framed in a flat tone he had never heard from her before.

Tension screaming from every line of his tall, powerful figure, Gio mounted the stairs a step in her harried wake. It was no comfort for him to flip through his list of sins and omissions with Billie because there were so many of them he didn't know where to start. He watched her stop dead in the living area of their suite and kick off her high heels, ensuring that she shrank greatly in stature.

Billie settled blazingly angry green eyes on Gio. 'Calisto told me that the pre-nup I signed contained something about you keeping Theo here in Greece if we broke up.'

Furious that something so highly confidential could have been leaked from what should have been the most trustworthy source, Gio turned pale, and for an instant he couldn't think of anything to say in his own defence.

Billie read his taut defensive expression and her shoulders slumped. 'So, it's true…this marriage has all been some cruel kind of game of deception.'

'The pre-nup no longer exists. I shredded your copy and mine and had my legal rep destroy all evidence of it,' Gio grated. 'It's gone, it's in the past. I should never have thought of such a thing.'

'How did you shred *my* copy?' Billie demanded in sudden wonderment.

'I went into your storage boxes,' Gio admitted, a tinge of heat accentuating his cheekbones at the look of disbelief growing in her gaze. 'I realised it was wrong and I wanted to destroy it. I didn't want you to realise what I'd tried to do at some later stage of our lives.'

'Well, you don't have that to worry about that now. It's come back to haunt you much sooner than you expected,' Billie pointed out, wondering how much she should be mollified by the apparent destruction of the document and his evident change of heart. At least he knew when he'd done something wrong, she thought limply, struggling to find a bright side to her predicament.

Gio studied her, his full attention locked to her flickering changes of expression. 'I didn't want to lose you.'

'You didn't want to lose Theo,' Billie corrected. 'I wish you'd just been honest from the beginning. I'm not unreasonable, Gio, and from the moment you reappeared I was willing to *share* Theo with you, honestly and fairly.'

'It was a very dirty trick to plant that clause in the pre-nup,' Gio acknowledged with a humility that astounded her.

'But very typical of you,' Billie responded. 'Clever, devious, cold-blooded.'

'I'm never cold-blooded when it comes to you. I had the pre-nup drawn up that way because...' Gio hesitated, lean, strong face rigid '...not because I was trying to take Theo off you, but because...'

'Because what?' Billie snapped in sudden frustration.

'Because I knew you'd never leave him and if I had the right to keep him, you wouldn't leave me either!' Gio yelled back at her full force, making her jump in fright.

Billie gaped at him. 'But I had no intention of leaving you.'

'You left me before!' Gio bit out rawly.

Billie stared at him, fighting to hide her fascination and astonishment. 'But don't you think there was some excuse for me leaving you then, when you were marrying another woman?' she reasoned very gently.

His lean, darkly handsome features froze as if she had slapped him. He released his breath in a long pent-up hiss. 'Marrying Calisto was the worst mistake I ever made...but I thought, I truly believed at the time that I was doing the right thing.'

Billie thought about what Theon had told her about the way he had raised Gio and the values he had emphasised and suppressed a sigh. 'But it wasn't the right thing for you.'

'I am so sorry for hurting you,' Gio framed in a roughened undertone, lustrous dark eyes unshielded and filled with overwhelming regret. 'If I could go back and change it, I would...but I can't. If it's any consolation, I hurt myself as well. For two years my life was miserable because you weren't part of it any longer, so I definitely paid for making the wrong choice. My happiest day since the day I lost you was the day when I finally found out where you were living.'

In her entire experience of Gio, Billie had never thought to hear such admissions from him. Initially the shock of what he was telling her almost struck her dumb and then the natural warmth of her nature sent her hurtling across the room to wrap both arms round him in comfort. 'Oh, Gio, you are an idiot sometimes,' she whispered helplessly.

'I honestly didn't believe you would leave me. When I found the apartment empty…well, it was a very bad moment for me and I did everything I could to fight feeling the way I did, but everything in my life felt wrong after that,' he confessed raggedly. 'Calisto got a bad deal from me as well. I didn't want her, I wanted you, and when you disappeared you were all I could think about.'

Belatedly Billie understood his ex-wife's hatred for her. 'Did she love you? She must've been jealous and hurt…'

'No, love wasn't part of our arrangement, nor was jealousy. If it had been she would never have agreed to me still keeping you in my life.'

'You *told* her about me? She actually agreed to you continuing to see me?' Billie prompted, shaken even though she recalled him saying something in that line before.

'I preferred to be honest with her from the start. Cal wanted social position. Her family are wealthy but have little status. She wanted to be Gio Letsos' wife for what it meant to the rest of the world. Unfortunately, I couldn't live with her,' Gio admitted with a grimace of recollection. 'She was nasty to my family and she lies at the drop of a hat about the most trivial things. After promising to have a family with me, she then confessed that she didn't *ever* want to have a child. In short, we were both dissatisfied with our marriage and she agreed to the divorce.'

'But then why is she carrying on this way trying to upset me and wreck our marriage?'

'I can only think I hurt her ego by not wanting her more than I wanted you. Obviously marrying you straight after the divorce offended her as well but we won't be having any more trouble from that quarter,' Gio asserted with conviction. 'That lawyer will be removed from my team and Leandros doesn't get on with Cal any better than I do, so there won't be any leaked info from him with regard to our lives.'

Ready to toss the issue of Calisto and his brief marriage on a back burner, Billie was instead thinking about what Gio had said about the pre-nup agreement he had had her sign. 'Why were you afraid of me leaving you again?' she murmured.

'My father left me, my mother left me and somehow you became even more important to me than they were,' Gio framed with dogged determination but obvious difficulty in explaining that to her. 'After I found my mother dead, I taught myself to close out emotions because it was the only way I could cope with the way my sisters' lives and mine had imploded. I preferred to stay in control. I felt threatened whenever emotion tried to take over. I found the way I seemed to *need* you totally unnerving...'

Billie was so stunned by that speech that the best she could manage was, 'Oh, dear...'

'I couldn't believe that you could try and send me away once I found you again.'

'Only because of Theo and I thought you'd be furious about him. And because you hurt me before and I didn't want to put myself out there for that again,' Billie told him truthfully.

'I did everything wrong, but then I would have done anything to get you back,' Gio confided. 'I shouldn't have used Dee's past as a weapon against you.'

'No, you shouldn't have.' Billie didn't pull her punches on that score. 'You blackmailed me into moving to your hotel!'

'I wanted you with me.'

'And then abandoned me at the hotel,' Billie reminded him stubbornly.

'My feelings around you were getting on top of me,' Gio breathed curtly. 'I couldn't handle them and I was getting angry and frustrated and I was afraid I might scare you off.'

'I didn't know you felt like that because until now you haven't shared anything with me,' she murmured ruefully.

Gio reached into his pocket and withdrew a ring

box, from which he removed a gleaming diamond solitaire. 'It's five minutes after midnight and your twenty-third birthday, *pethi mou*. Happy birthday.' He lifted her hand and threaded the beautiful ring onto her wedding finger. 'It belonged to my grandmother and now it belongs to you. They enjoyed a very long and happy marriage; consequently it comes with a worthy history for us to follow.'

Billie gazed down at her beautiful ring with tears of joy glittering in her eyes because that family gift meant so much more to her than a ring that he might have bought.

'I should have placed that ring on your finger two years ago but I didn't know my own heart then,' Gio confessed heavily. 'I had never stopped to evaluate what you actually meant to me and by the time that I did, it was too late and you were gone. Even after I found you again and married you, I genuinely *still* didn't appreciate that what I feel for you has to be love.'

'Love?' Billie exclaimed, jolted by surprise from her blissful perusal of her engagement ring.

'I do love you,' Gio declared with an endearing amount of self-consciousness about making such a statement. 'I probably always loved you but it was a very selfish love, so I didn't recognise it for what it was and neither could you have done.'

Billie was bemused. 'Gio…you just called yourself selfish…'

Gio frowned. 'I couldn't avoid that deduction after I found your exam certificates and all the courses which you had done while we were together two years back... I didn't know about even *one* of them,' he decried. 'I wish you'd told me.'

Billie was flushed. 'I was too embarrassed. You have a degree and there I was studying for the most basic qualifications,' she pointed out. 'My goodness, is that why you took me to that stupid art gallery tonight?'

'I thought you'd enjoy it,' Gio admitted.

'I only took the course because of that Canaletto thing,' she muttered ruefully. 'But to be frank, it's all a bit highbrow for me.'

'I'm not into art either. I wouldn't change a single thing about you. I'm proud of you and happy to show you off anywhere. I'm *really* proud that you're my wife,' Gio imparted with a brilliant beautiful smile as he scooped her up in his arms and carried her through to their bed.

'Honestly?' Billie pressed.

'Honestly,' Gio stressed. 'I only wish I'd understood the strength of what I felt for you a lot sooner because it would have saved us both a great deal of unhappiness. I would never willingly have let you go.'

'I still love you,' Billie told him with a forgiving grin that illuminated her whole face.

'I have to wonder why,' he said seriously.

'Maybe because I see a side of you that other people don't. I don't know. I just always loved you,' Billie mused, relaxed about her own feelings for the first time in years because he loved her back. A singing, dizzy sense of happiness was spreading through her, all her fears finally laid to rest.

'Bet I love you even more than you love me,' Gio husked, dark eyes smouldering gold as he kissed her with sweet, ravishing hunger. 'I'm hopelessly competitive.'

'You can win that competition any time you like,' Billie joked, feeling gloriously free to express her own feelings as she gripped his shirt collar and dragged him down to her again.

Billie watched Theo race into the waves with Jade and Davis while Gio kept a watch on the children.

'You know,' Dee remarked from her lounger by Billie's side on the deck of the beach house, 'Gio's totally different from the sort of man I thought he was. He's great with kids, for a start.'

'Oh, he's surprised me too in that line,' Billie confided lazily, her attention on the six-month-old daughter sleeping in her portable crib in the shadows. 'He adores Ianthe.'

'When does your family tree get a look-in with the names?' Dee asked.

'Are you joking?' Billie laughed. 'With Grandpa being a Wilfred and Grandma Ethel, I think Gio's family names have more promise. What were we talking about? Right, yes, Gio and children. He's surprised too by how much he enjoys having a family.'

'Billie, if you wanted a giraffe in the family, he'd try to give it to you,' her cousin said with a roll of her eyes. 'The man is besotted. I can see it every time he looks at you.'

'Maybe it'll be your turn soon,' Billie remarked quietly, because Dee had started seeing someone back home. It was early days yet, of course, but she was hoping Dee would be brave enough to try another relationship because her cousin spent too much time alone.

It had been two years since Billie had married Gio and Dee was currently in the process of buying Billie's vintage clothes shop, which she was still successfully managing. A lot had changed for Billie in that same period but Gio had changed too, opening up to his emotions and pulling free of an outlook that had once been set in stone. He would never be Dee's best friend but he could relax now with the other woman and accept her place in Billie's life without comment or tension. Billie suspected that their children had helped Gio become more relaxed and flexible.

Theo was tall for a three-year-old, like all the men in the Letsos family, and he had Gio's black hair messily combined with his mother's corkscrew curls, something he would no doubt complain bitterly about when he reached his teenaged years, Billie reflected fondly. Ianthe was a combination of their genes as well, for her eyes had turned as green as her mother's and she was fairer in colouring than her brother with dead straight hair with not even a hint of a curl.

Billie went into the beach house for a cold drink

and glanced around with a rather wicked smile because she knew that she and Gio would be spending the night there. Dee and the children were heading home in the afternoon and Irene, their trusty nanny, would collect Theo and Ianthe to take them back to the villa.

In the two years since she had married Gio, Billie had learned to make the most of their private time together. Gio travelled less than he once had and their lives were based on the island. Billie got on great with Gio's family and was particularly close to his sisters and never short of company. Sometimes she wanted to pinch herself because she had never dreamt that she could be so happy.

A pair of arms closed round her from behind and she jumped. *'Gio?'*

'Who else?' he breathed teasingly above her head.

'You gave me a fright,' she whispered, swivelling round in his arms to look up at him. 'Who's with the children?'

'Dee's taking a turn.'

Billie collided with smouldering dark golden eyes set in a stunning lean dark face and wrapped her arms round his neck, her heart hammering. 'You still rock my world, Mr Letsos,' she confided breathlessly.

Gio dealt her a thrillingly erotic smile of anticipation. 'Not until tonight, *agapi mou.*'

He called her 'my love' now, Billie reflected blissfully, for she now spoke a fair amount of Greek. Her curvaceous body sealed slowly to his with intense appreciation of the strength and protectiveness in his tall, well-built length. 'I love you, Gio…'

'And I am totally devoted to you,' Gio intoned huskily, bending his head to steal a kiss that went on until they had to break apart to breathe.

* * * * *

COMING NEXT MONTH FROM

HARLEQUIN

Presents®

Available January 20, 2015

#3305 DELUCCA'S MARRIAGE CONTRACT

The Chatsfield

by Abby Green

Happily ever after was never part of this business arrangement, but Giancarlo Delucca finds himself intrigued by his bride Keelin O'Connor's feisty defiance. Now he's determined to turn the beautiful heiress's "I don't" into an "I do"!

#3306 THE REDEMPTION OF DARIUS STERNE

The Twin Tycoons

by Carole Mortimer

Virginal Miranda can't resist the allure of billionaire Darius Sterne. But the closer Darius pulls her, the more he threatens the barriers that conceal the scars of her past. Yet Miranda isn't the only one with pain to hide...

#3307 PLAYING BY THE GREEK'S RULES

by Sarah Morgan

Nik Zervakis lives by his own tenets, and there's no one better to teach Lily Rose how to separate sizzling sex from deep emotions. It starts as a sensual game, but can Lily stick to Nik's rules? And can he?

#3308 THE SULTAN'S HAREM BRIDE

Desert Vows

by Annie West

Journalist Jacqui Fletcher jumps at the chance to write a history of the harem—not to become a sultan's plaything! But it's hard to remember her assignment when Asim of Jazeer's sensuous caresses spark a fire she's never experienced before...

HPCNM0115RA

#3309 TO WEAR HIS RING AGAIN
by Chantelle Shaw
When Isobel sees her husband, Constantin de Severino, again, the temptation to wear his ring once more becomes overwhelming. But as long-dormant secrets are uncovered, Isobel must decide if Constantin is still hers to have and to hold...

#3310 INNOCENT IN HIS DIAMONDS
by Maya Blake
CEO Bastien Heidecker holds Ana Duval's family responsible for the destruction of his own. So he'll satisfy his craving for her, then discard her. But what happens when he discovers that Ana is innocent in *every* sense of the word?

#3311 THE MAN TO BE RECKONED WITH
by Tara Pammi
Even though he's furious that Riya has brought him back to face his past, Nathanial Ramirez can't refuse her bait. Now he'll use every sensual weapon in his considerable arsenal to secure his heritage...and get Riya in his bed!

#3312 CLAIMED BY THE SHEIKH
by Rachael Thomas
Prince Kazim banished his wife from his kingdom long ago but now he needs her back. Amber's always threatened Kazim's tightly held control, yet to save his nation—and his marriage—he must finally make the ultimate claim...on his wife!

REQUEST YOUR FREE BOOKS!

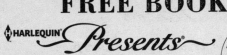

2 FREE NOVELS PLUS
2 FREE GIFTS!

YES! Please send me 2 FREE Harlequin Presents® novels and my 2 FREE gifts (gifts are worth about $10). After receiving them, if I don't wish to receive any more books, I can return the shipping statement marked "cancel." If I don't cancel, I will receive 6 brand-new novels every month and be billed just $4.30 per book in the U.S. or $4.99 per book in Canada. That's a saving of at least 14% off the cover price! It's quite a bargain! Shipping and handling is just 50¢ per book in the U.S. and 75¢ per book in Canada.* I understand that accepting the 2 free books and gifts places me under no obligation to buy anything. I can always return a shipment and cancel at any time. Even if I never buy another book, the two free books and gifts are mine to keep forever.

106/306 HDN FVRK

Name	(PLEASE PRINT)

Address	Apt. #

City	State/Prov.	Zip/Postal Code

Signature (if under 18, a parent or guardian must sign)

Mail to the Harlequin® Reader Service:
IN U.S.A.: P.O. Box 1867, Buffalo, NY 14240-1867
IN CANADA: P.O. Box 609, Fort Erie, Ontario L2A 5X3

**Are you a current subscriber to Harlequin Presents books
and want to receive the larger-print edition?
Call 1-800-873-8635 or visit www.ReaderService.com.**

* Terms and prices subject to change without notice. Prices do not include applicable taxes. Sales tax applicable in N.Y. Canadian residents will be charged applicable taxes. Offer not valid in Quebec. This offer is limited to one order per household. Not valid for current subscribers to Harlequin Presents books. All orders subject to credit approval. Credit or debit balances in a customer's account(s) may be offset by any other outstanding balance owed by or to the customer. Please allow 4 to 6 weeks for delivery. Offer available while quantities last.

Your Privacy—The Harlequin® Reader Service is committed to protecting your privacy. Our Privacy Policy is available online at www.ReaderService.com or upon request from the Harlequin Reader Service.

We make a portion of our mailing list available to reputable third parties that offer products we believe may interest you. If you prefer that we not exchange your name with third parties, or if you wish to clarify or modify your communication preferences, please visit us at www.ReaderService.com/consumerschoice or write to us at Harlequin Reader Service Preference Service, P.O. Box 9062, Buffalo, NY 14269. Include your complete name and address.

* * *

"It's true that if you turn up as my guest tonight there
will be people who assume we are having sex." Nik
returned his attention to the conversation. "I can't claim
to be intimately acquainted with the guest list, but I'm
assuming a few of the people there will be your colleagues. Does that bother you?"

"No. It will send a message that I'm not brokenhearted,
which is good for my pride. In fact the timing is perfect.
Just this morning I embarked on a new project. Operation
Ice Maiden. You're probably wondering what that is."

Nik opened his mouth to comment but she carried on
without pausing.

"I am going to have sex with no emotion. That's right."
She nodded at him. "You heard me correctly. Rebound
sex. I am going to climb into bed with some guy and I'm
not going to feel a thing."

Hearing a sound from the front of the car, Nik pressed a button and closed the screen between him and Vassilis, giving them privacy.

"Do you have anyone in mind for—er—Operation Ice Maiden?"

"Not yet, but if they happen to think it's you that's fine. You'd look good on my romantic résumé."

Nik leaned his head back against the seat and started to laugh. "You, Lily, are priceless."

"That doesn't sound like a compliment." She adjusted the neckline of her dress and her breasts almost escaped in the process.

Dragging his gaze from her body, Nik decided this was the most entertaining evening he'd had in a long time… and the night was still young.

* * *

It starts as a sensual game,
but can Lily stick to Nik's rules?
And what's more, can he…?

Find out in:
PLAYING BY THE GREEK'S RULES
February 2015

www.Harlequin.com

HPEXP0115-1

HARLEQUIN

Presents®

Abby Green

brings you a sensational story full of passion and excitement!

DELUCCA'S MARRIAGE CONTRACT

February 2015

Happily-ever-after was never part of this business arrangement, but Giancarlo Delucca finds himself intrigued by his bride, Keelin O'Connor's, feisty defiance. Now he's determined to turn the beautiful heiress's "I don't" into an "I do"!

Harlequin Presents welcomes you to the world of *The Chatsfield:*

Synonymous with style, spectacle…and scandal!

Love the Harlequin book you just read?

Your opinion matters.

Review this book on your favorite book site, review site, blog or your own social media properties and share your opinion with other readers!

Be sure to connect with us at:
Harlequin.com/Newsletters
Facebook.com/HarlequinBooks
Twitter.com/HarlequinBooks

JUST CAN'T GET ENOUGH
ROMANCE

Looking for more?

Harlequin has everything from contemporary, passionate and heartwarming to suspenseful and inspirational stories.

Whatever your mood,
we have a romance just for you!

Connect with us to find your next great read,
special offers and more.

Facebook.com/HarlequinBooks
Twitter.com/HarlequinBooks
HarlequinBlog.com
Harlequin.com/Newsletters

HARLEQUIN®

A *Romance* FOR EVERY MOOD™

www.Harlequin.com